MW01129475

Taste of Vengeance

Gia Santella Crime Thrillers, Volume 6

Kristi Belcamino

Published by Kristi Belcamino, 2018.

TASTE OF VENGEANCE

First edition. August 16, 2018.

Written by Kristi Belcamino.

La vendetta è mia. Vengeance is mine—
Deuteronomy 32:35

TASTE OF VENGEANCE

Kristi Belcamino

PROLOGUE

R*io de Janiero
Carnival*

Every which way I turned, it seemed there was a masked figure leering at me, reaching for me, hands and eyes and mouths stretching and elongating to the throbbing beat of the samba music.

Fingers caressed me intimately as I squeezed my frame through the mass of bodies swelling the street. I shrank from the inevitable petting, a cupped hand reaching to fondle my breast, a lingering caress. My nerves were electric, my body tense as I imagined the cool blade of a knife sliding between my rib case. As I wove through the crowd, a popping sound made me jump. It was all too easy to imagine the crack of fireworks as a volley of gunfire. I kept walking. I didn't have time to fight off the sensual assault coming at me from all sides. I could only hope the man who hunted me wasn't the next body I brushed against.

The pulsating, movement of the parade gave me more refuge than the sidewalks, where someone running among the stationary spectators would attract attention. That type of exposure could be fatal. So, I ran into the thicket of bodies. I bore the stroking of strangers, slipping through the squirming mass, emerging slick with their sweat only to be embraced by the next clump of costumed humanity.

Ahead, I could see a massive float spreading across the entire street. To get around it, I'd have to mingle with the crowd on the sidewalks. I'd have to take my chances.

That became clearer when the parade abruptly ground to a halt for the start of a new samba school performance.

Afraid to move my head and attract attention, I strained to see, using my peripheral vision to scan the crowd. Out of the corner of my eye I saw a tall figure I would've recognized anywhere. He was headed my way.

Despite the *bauta* mask—a white grotesque face with a large nose, no mouth, and creepy beak-like chin—I knew it was him.

At that moment, he looked up and our eyes met. Both of us masked but instantly recognizing one another.

We held each other's gaze for a second before I darted, toppling people as I went, throwing apologies over my shoulder as I created a human domino effect to stop the man trying to kill me.

I reached the sidewalk and paused. A door lay before me, but it could be locked. To the right of the door was a passageway. But it could be a dead end.

There was no time for indecision so I started toward the passageway. Before I could take a step, I felt cold steel on my neck.

I'd run out of time.

CHAPTER ONE-
Bitterly cold

B*efore ...*
Ocean Beach, San Francisco

Sydney Rye woke at dawn so she could take Blue for a run before anyone else hit the beach and could bitch about leash laws. She wasn't sure what the rules were in San Francisco so it was best to avoid anyone else out running for now.

Without turning on any lights in the small cottage, she did a series of stretches and a smattering of yoga.

Blue stretched beside her, mimicking a few of the poses. He was a Great Dane-sized dog with the furry white coat of a wolf and a Collie's nose.

Sydney tugged a black fleece jacket on over the layers she'd already donned. Today would involve a shopping trip for warmer clothes. The bitterly cold wind pierced right through the clothes she'd brought from the tropical island headquarters of Joyful Justice. When she'd flown in late last night, she'd shivered the entire ride from the airport to the beachfront rental.

But she was used to missions and leads that sent her around the world. Syria. India. Mexico.

She'd lived in caves, tents, motorhomes.

San Francisco was posh in comparison.

5

Her latest mission was to find a San Francisco woman who had last been seen partying in Rio with some Silicon Valley big shots. A family attorney had contacted Joyful Justice saying that Alaia Schwartz was missing and he believed she might be the most recent in a string of missing Bay Area women. That piqued Sydney's interest.

When Sydney learned the names of the Silicon Valley luminaries the woman had last been with—Damien Thornwell and Richard Zimmer–she'd arranged a "chance" meeting with the men at the Cannes Film Festival.

While there, Sydney finagled a dinner seat next to Thornwell. During small talk, he asked what she did. She made up a story about a business she thought would interest him—high-tech developments in private security forces.

She left France with an invitation to call on him when she so *coincidentally* happened to be attending a meeting in San Francisco a few weeks later.

As she ran along the San Francisco beach, Sydney received the text she'd been waiting for from Dan at headquarters.

"The caretaker is waiting for you at the Schwartz house. I told him to expect you there this morning," the text said.

"Thanks," she wrote back and thought, *caretaker?*

SYDNEY DOUBLE-CHECKED the address before she lifted the huge Gargoyle knocker. The brass thudded dully on the wooden door. Blue looked up at her expectantly.

The Pacific Heights neighborhood perched on the north side of San Francisco. The drive over had revealed spectacular views of the Golden Gate Bridge as the sun rose casting the iconic landmark in a pinkish orange light. The neighborhood was old money. Huge mansions crammed onto tiny lots.

She waited for somebody to answer the door.

Nobody came. She lifted the knocker again, but put it back down gently. That wasn't going to work. The surrounding walls were enveloped by trailing branches of ivy. There had to be some type of doorbell somewhere. She lifted one branch to the right. A white intercom lay beneath.

She pushed the button.

"Schwartz residence."

"It's Sydney Rye."

The door clicked open with a buzzing sound. She waited and then pushed it open with the toe of her shoe a few inches, revealing a slice of Persian carpet.

A second later, the heavy door swung open, and a man stood there blinking. He was balding with a paunch and wore black pants, a white shirt, and a black vest.

"I'm Cyril. Ms. Schwartz' manservant."

Sydney bit back her retort and settled on a simple smile.

The man jumped when he noticed Blue.

"Don't worry. He won't bite."

Cyril pursed his lips in disapproval.

"Really," Sydney said.

Exhaling loudly, Cyril shook his head. "When Mr. Schwartz was alive, animals were not allowed, but I suppose we could make an exception today."

Blue loped in beside her. He touched his nose to her thigh—a gentle tap to let her know he was there.

After Cyril shut the door behind her, he turned and walked down the hall, speaking over his shoulder.

"We are besides ourselves with worry. I hope you can find her."

We? The royal we? Or did he mean himself and the family attorney?

As they passed open doorways, Sydney peered inside. Old money. Old everything. It didn't seem like the home of a twenty-three-year-old heiress.

They reached a kitchen area—obviously, Cyril's part of the house. A small table was pushed in one corner with a Dashiell Hammett paperback splayed open.

"I just made some tea and mini *croque-monsieurs*. We will take them in the sitting room." He grabbed a tray and kept walking.

Sydney, with Blue pressed close, followed him into an alcove containing an upholstered couch, love seat, and chair. Where they weren't covered with massive oil paintings, the walls radiated a peaceful buttercup yellow.

Very. Old. Money.

Cyril settled into an armchair in the far corner, placing the tray on the coffee table.

Sydney settled on the edge of the loveseat closest to the chair. Blue sprawled at her feet. She reached for a *croque-monsieurs*, took a bite, and then dropped the rest at her feet. Blue swallowed it whole. When she saw the horrified expression on Cyril's face, she was secretly pleased.

"Sorry, he didn't have much breakfast. We got in late last night and I haven't had time to buy dog food."

Cyril nodded and swallowed. He handed her a small white cloth napkin. Sydney realized she had dropped a crumb on the coffee table. She placed it in the napkin and leaned back in her seat. *Manservant. More like uptight baby man.*

"Has Alaia lived here long?"

Cyril paused. He blinked rapidly. "She only moved back when her father, Mr. Schwartz, passed last December." A small tear dropped down one cheek. He didn't bother to wipe it.

Two months.

"Pardon me," he said. "If you count when she returned from Europe to be with him during his final days, it would be more like November."

Three months.

Alaia had not only inherited the house—she'd apparently inherited Cyril.

"How long did you work for Mr. Schwartz?" Sydney asked and took a sip of her tea. Mint. Surprisingly good.

Cyril sighed and shook his head, pressing his lips together. He fanned his eyes with his hands to prevent the tears. It didn't work. "I'm sorry. It's really hard." His voice was thick with emotion. "I was with Mr. Schwartz for twenty years."

"I'm so sorry," Sydney said.

He sniffled and nodded his thanks.

"What can you tell me about Alaia and the last time you saw her."

He blew out air loudly. "Honestly? She told me to take a vacation. That she really didn't need me. She didn't want me to fix dinner. She didn't want me to make tea. Frankly, I've felt completely and utterly useless..."

"What will you do now?"

"Mr. Schwartz made provisions in his will that I can remain here for as long as I live."

"That was generous."

He sat up straight and frowned. "I took care of that man for twenty years. I clipped his toenails. I even, when he was ill, tended to his business after he was done on the toilet. I don't think it is too much to ask to not be kicked out of my home."

"Hold up, cowboy. I think you took that completely wrong," Sydney said. "It's my job to figure all this out and ask questions"

He sat back and she pressed on.

"Did the will stipulate that Alaia couldn't sell the house?"

"That's right." He settled back, seemingly pacified by her comment.

If she were a detective, Sydney knew she should instantly consider Old Manservant Cyril a suspect. Kill the pesky daughter. Live alone in a mansion in Pacific Heights until he died. Jackpot. But it didn't feel right. Cyril seemed incapable of killing a mouse. He'd be the one up on a chair screaming and cowering. But who knew? She wasn't ready to rule him out, yet, but he didn't feel good for it. Other theories, like something fishy with the Silicon Valley crowd, was a better bet.

She put down her cup. She didn't really have time for any more niceties. She stood. Blue followed suit.

"Can you show me her room?"

That's why she was here, after all. She didn't think Cyril could provide much detail in how or why Alaia disappeared. Unless he had killed her. And she'd circle back around if that started to seem likely.

Cyril smoothed his pants legs as he stood. "There are eight guest rooms in this home. And yet, Alaia decided that she wanted to sleep in the cabana by the pool." He clucked his disdain.

Sydney had expected to be taken outside—hadn't he said "pool?"—but instead Cyril led her past a wall of windows that overlooked a massive indoor pool below. The ceiling was made of an elaborate domed skylight.

Cyril pushed the button for an elevator. Sydney balked. "It's just one flight down. Are there stairs?"

The elevator door slid open revealing a gold phone attached to the wall. He held his arm out for her to go first. Internally shrugging, she stepped inside with Blue at her heels.

Inside the elevator, the lighting was dim. A small, red velvet covered bench was pressed against one wall. Cyril stood pressed against the door, as far away from Blue as he could get.

Sydney jutted her chin at the phone. "Does it work?"

Cyril lifted the receiver to her ear. There was a dial tone. He smiled and hung it back up.

The elevator doors slid open to reveal the pool area. She and Blue followed Cyril along the Italian tiles surrounding the pool to a large free-standing building on the opposite side of the massive space. The cabana.

Cyril flung open the door and then leaned over to flick a light switch. Sydney's first impression was that it was a room full of clothes and nothing else. "I haven't touched it since she disappeared," Cyril said, wrinkling his nose. "Take the elevator back up to the second floor when you are finished and I will see you out." He gave Blue a wary glance. "Does he need to use the facilities?"

It took her a minute to figure out what the hell the man was talking about.

"He's fine. Thanks, Cyril," Sydney said, tempted to punch him in the shoulder and call him "Old chap." *Manservant. How archaic could you get?*

Before she stepped inside, Sydney paused, trying to gather a first impression of the girl who had lived here for three months. The photos she'd been sent showed a young woman with dark hair and striking green eyes against olive skin. Her buxom figure was draped in flowing, bright clothing. The floor of the cabana reflected her flamboyant style. A small twin mattress was pushed up against one wall. Everything was bathed in an otherworldly light from the reflection of the blue pool water that seeped in through filmy white curtains.

An open doorway revealed a small bathroom and counter lined with cosmetics and beauty products. The room smelled both exotic and sweet—a mix of tangerine and spice and vanilla.

A tidy row of books, spines facing out, rested against the wall near the head of the mattress. *Siddhartha. The Four-Hour Work Week. Boss Babe Manifesto.* Taking it all in with a glance, Sydney nodded to herself.

The report from the family attorney had said that Alaia was looking for an investor for a new business venture. She was developing a device—a mobile pod—that would be placed at public locations, such as parks and shopping center, that could scan bodies and immediately send a health report to a doctor or hospital.

Her father's will had stipulated that once she made her first million, she would inherit the fortune he'd left for her. But until then, the only provisions his will had made for her was house and board.

On the bed, a three-ring notebook was open.

At first, as she made her way over to the bed, Sydney tried not to step on the clothes, but quickly gave up. She eased herself down on the bed, imagining that this was where Alaia sat when she wrote in her notebook. Sydney nodded at Blue—who laid down at the entrance, putting his chin on his paws watching her—and began to read.

CHAPTER TWO-
Losing Control

March 2001

M He squeezed more lotion onto his palm. His hand worked his cock in a frenzy. The image on his computer screen had sent him into a tizzy. It'd been easy to gain access to her computer.

Stupid bitch didn't know that the small round camera perched on top of her monitor allowed him a full peep show to her entire life. He'd given her the camera, that was affixed to the top of her monitor, and helped her install it, saying she would then be able to speak to her foreign exchange student friend in France. She'd been wary but grateful. Her computer rested on her dresser and gave him a full view of her room. It was also right in front of her mirror.

Right now, that meant a front-row seat of her spectacular tits as she jiggled them in her palms, looking at herself in the mirror and making faces. She practiced seductive poses. It sent him into a frenzy. His slippery hand moved faster, sliding up and down until his eyes rolled back in ecstasy.

She was out of his league. He knew this. But he still could have her. At least online. And one day, when he was rich and powerful, he'd have women like her every single day.

He'd just finished wiping himself when his door swung open. His mother stood in the doorway holding a sledge hammer. She'd knocked the doorknob right off the door. He pushed his headphones down around his neck.

Scrambling, he tried to hide himself, but his pants were open wide, and his cock stood at attention. His mother's eyes went to the computer screen before him, but he'd instantly clicked a button so the screen showed a video game. Hiding the picture of Lila Grant had been more important than hiding his erect penis.

"Oh, my God. What are you doing?" His mom was horrified. The look on her face. It was if she'd just walked into a bloody murder scene. She stood there in the doorway, sweaty and panting.

"What's it look like?" he said.

"This is what you do all day in here? You ... you play with yourself?"

"It's called masturbation. It's natural."

"There is nothing natural about it." Her voice rose in a shriek. "I have been calling you to dinner, pounding, screaming at you to unlock the door, for the past thirty minutes."

He didn't answer.

"You're lucky I don't take this hammer to all of your precious equipment." Her voice was shrill.

He stood, fury surging through him. He felt his face grow hot and his wrath building, rising. He was losing control. He started toward his mother, arm outstretched, finger pointing at her, his entire body shaking with rage.

"Get out. Get out. Get out." With each reiteration of the phrase, his voice grew lower. The white calmness of his emotion made his mother's eyes grow wide. She opened her mouth as if to speak, but instead it opened and closed like a guppy sucking for air. But she didn't budge.

He'd stood and walked over to her, grabbing her by the neck. He put his face close to hers. The year he'd turned sixteen was also the year he'd grown as tall as her. He drew close and hissed the words, spittle flying onto her cheeks. "You won't touch anything in here." He waited.

Her eyes grew wide. "In fact, if you ever step foot in this room again, I will wait until you are asleep, and I will take your sledge hammer to your skull. Do you understand?"

She swallowed and nodded.

"Leave. Now."

She backed out of the room.

The door swung closed behind her. A small circle of light shone where the doorknob had once been.

For a few seconds, he allowed the anger to fill his limbs. He'd use that rage as fuel to create something the world had never seen before. To make him so powerful that he'd never again live in a room where he couldn't bar the door. One day, he and Damien would rule the world. They would have every woman they wanted begging to suck their cocks. It was just a matter of time. It would start here—in this room. This tiny garage space he'd converted to a hacker's paradise was where it would all begin.

CHAPTER THREE-
Cuddle Puddle

As Sydney read on, Alaia's journal pointed in one direction and it wasn't to the effeminate manservant, Cyril.

The journal entries told of a world of sex parties where the Silicon Valley crowd did most of its business.

According to Alaia's journal, there were two types of parties hosted by the founders–the creators of the billion-dollar tech companies and the venture capitalists—known as the V.C.'s.

One type of party was strictly for the "tech elite"—the first investors, the heavy hitters, the deal makers. It was the other type that Alaia talked about the most—the parties with more women than men. The "hot ticket" private parties. If you were a woman in tech invited to one of these parties you might as well move back to the Midwest.

Because you couldn't win.

If you attended a party, you were considered a slut and not taken seriously. Not going meant you'd be shunned in Silicon Valley's close-knit community.

According to Alaia, the latter type party often had a theme. Sometimes it was pure sex, where drugs and alcohol were banned to promote safe behavior. At those, attendees would peel off into bedrooms either as a pair or a group. Sometime the parties were strictly about getting high, where everyone would sit around and take MDMA, called Molly, or other drugs. But most often it was a combination of the two.

But Alaia knew none of this when a woman from Zimmer's office called her. "There's this party—invite only—and Rich wanted me to invite you."

Well, if Richard Zimmer wanted her there, Alaia thought she should probably go. The last meeting she'd had with him, she'd caught him leering at her under his hooded eyes. But he'd said he was very interested in investing in her idea. He'd just have to talk Damien Thornwell, his partner, into it.

Alaia knew she *had* to show at the party. It wasn't an invite—it was a summons.

But the then woman who had issued the invite had hinted at something else. "The party has a theme—bondage," she'd said.

"Oh, fun," Alaia had said, thinking it was like a costume party.

But now at the party, it didn't take long for her to realize that couples were disappearing from the main room. Zimmer had a huge great room that was filled with candles and strewn with velvet pillows and fluffy blankets. Because there wasn't any furniture, people had no choice but to lounge on the pillows on the floor, Alaia wrote. Soon, hands wandered. The man and woman on each side of her—an older married couple in their late thirties—began stroking her thighs, her hair, and her arms.

At that point, she was sleepy lazy and high from the Molly someone had handed her. The caresses felt good. At the same time, her brain screamed that this wasn't cool. The married couple was sure to resent her and punish her for this the next day when everyone was stone cold sober. Plus, she fully wasn't into women. She'd tried sleeping with her roommate in college for kicks, and they'd both decided that bisexuality wasn't for them.

This couple had sort of grossed her out, too. I mean, maybe the woman was a little old for the leather thigh-high boots and mini skirt. She was thin, but her outfit revealed flabby and wrinkly skin.

Alaia tried to brush off the couple, but then the man had pulled her down and began kissing her. She fought to get away, but found the wife pressing on top of her from above. When she finally broke free, she jumped up and ran away, breathing heavy and shaking. Nobody even looked up.

As she walked past, one woman stopped her.

"Do you want to join our cuddle puddle?"

Alaia was confused and then looked to where the woman pointed. Five people were on the floor entwined, stroking and kissing one another.

Shaking her head, Alaia kept walking. That's when she saw Richard Zimmer standing in the shadows, watching. He slowly raised his crystal tumbler to her and then turned on his heel, looking back to make sure she knew she should follow him, Alaia wrote.

Sydney could guess what happened next but she kept reading.

But as Sydney read on, she realized that Alaia had refused to sleep with Zimmer. She'd taken one look at the bedroom where he'd led her and left the party.

"Bravo," Sydney said and flipped forward in the notebook.

"It's bullshit," Alaia wrote. "I'm going to secretly record everything and expose these people. They can't do this. I'll sell it all to the tabloids, or better yet, get on Oprah and then get a book deal. I've tried, but I'm not cut out to run a business. My dad is wrong. I will never be like him. I tried. I really did. I have a solid business plan. Solid enough that Damien Thornwell and Richard Zimmer expressed interest. I know they really think it's a good plan and don't just want to fuck me. But unfortunately, the sex seems to go with the whole deal. And the drugs."

On the next page, Alaia seemed to have changed her mind.

"Zimmer wants to meet," she wrote. "Says he owes me an apology. Damn right he does. And that he has a check made out to me. For three million dollars. He's going to give it to me on our trip to Rio. He said he can't live with himself unless I go. Damien even called and insisted I let them make it up to me with the all-expenses paid trip. They said it's the chance of a lifetime to see the city the way they know it."

Sydney stared at the words.

She'd been waiting for the Rio connection.

The folder Sydney had been given on Alaia had contained a cryptic text the woman had sent. It had been the last time she'd ever been heard from. It said: "Rio. *Pied-à-terre*. Love pills. Notebook."

Quickly flipping the page of the woman's journal, Sydney looked for more information on the Rio trip, but there were only blank pages.

In her heart, she knew the answers lay in Rio, but right now she'd stick to her strongest lead—the two men Alaia was last seen with.

Grabbing her phone, she texted Thornwell.

"It's Sydney Rye. I'm in the city. Ready to take you up on your offer to show me around."

Within ten minutes she had a party invite for that night.

When she mentioned she was worried about leaving Blue alone in the rental cottage at the beach, Thornwell responded immediately, "Bring him. My dog would love the company."

Perfect.

CHAPTER FOUR-
Like it Rough

San Mateo County, California

S
He closed the distance between us, snaking through the crowd effortlessly. Bodies parted, jeweled women smiled longingly at him, tuxedoed men nodded respectfully. Candles flickered as he strode past. He left a wake of gawkers in his intensity to get to me.

His eyes locked onto mine. He wasn't terribly good looking. It was more that he exuded something irresistible. Confidence. Swagger. A presence like none I'd ever felt.

"Gia?" Dante's voice at my side came to me as if it was underwater. I barely registered the words from my best friend as the man grew closer, eyes trained on me.

Something in the man's scrutiny was both exciting and dangerous.

Damien. That was what Dante had said before the blood thrumming in my ears drowned him out. His name was Damien. Another goddamn "D" person. I attracted them as if I possessed a magnetic charge. What was up with that?

At first, I'd been delighted that he'd singled me out before I'd barely stepped foot into the party, but the closer he got, the more alarmed I became. I didn't believe in fate—or destiny, or, soul mates, for fuck's sake—but I couldn't deny that something life-changing was happening.

The thought sent a rush of adrenaline and fear pulsing through me. My smile faded.

He was still twenty feet away when my fight-or-flight instinct kicked in.

I turned and fled.

I heard Dante calling after me, but I didn't even pause.

I searched for the front door, having difficulty navigating through the sprawling house.

As I tried to find the exit, I took a wrong turn in the candlelit hallways. I didn't see a man step out of a dark doorway until I nearly collided with him. I was about to apologize, when he grabbed my wrists in a vice-like grip. "You like it rough?"

An icy chill ran through me at his touch. I wrenched myself out of his grip easily, but he stepped forward, pushing me toward the open doorway. "You are the most spankable woman in this town."

For a split second, I pondered how that sentence could possibly be considered a turn-on but forgot about it as my knee met his crotch. He doubled over and groaned just as a group of women rounded the corner.

"Which way is the front door?" I asked the women, taking them in. One woman wore thigh-high boots, a corset, and held a black leather whip by her side.

The other woman, wearing a studded collar, pointed wordlessly toward the other end of the hall. I raced to the front door, eager to get the hell out of this city and back to my-own-brand-of-weird San Francisco neighborhood.

It was only when I'd reached my Ferrari parked in the driveway near the other luxury cars, that I dared to take a breath. Once I was inside my car with my door firmly shut, I looked back at the house. A dark figure stood at the top of the stairs.

I gunned my engine and left a patch of rubber on the cobblestoned driveway. I kept my eyes on the rearview mirror until his silhouette became a pinprick. He never moved.

CHAPTER FIVE-
Doppelganger

Sydney Rye watched the dark-haired woman pause in the doorway of the party.

For a second, Sydney was taken aback. But then she realized she was wrong. It was not Alaia. But the brunette was the spitting image of the missing woman.

It was only when the woman turned to her companion, an attractive man with black hair and olive skin, that Sydney realized it was definitely a different person.

This woman had black eyes, not green like Alaia. She was also taller. The description of Alaia pegged her at five-foot-two. This woman was several inches taller than that. And while they were both curvy, this woman seemed a little less buxom than Alaia's photo revealed.

However, before she had a chance to think about it more, the woman turned and fled. Sydney's eyes searched the room. Damien Thornwell was heading toward the doorway where the woman had once stood.

It took Thornwell a few seconds to make his way through the crowd. He brushed past people, including the woman's companion, and disappeared out the door of the living room.

Sydney was tempted to follow, but knew that would seem suspicious, especially since Richard Zimmer had just taken her drink order and was making his way across the room, holding her tequila gimlet aloft.

Her best bet in finding out information on Alaia would be to stick close to Zimmer.

The night was young.

CHAPTER SIX-
Star Struck

"You suck."

Dante didn't usually deign to use vulgar words like that. He must be really angry.

"That's not fair." I was huddled on the floor of my loft, my back pressed against the wall of mirrors I used for my Budo training. My beautiful dress was crumpled around me, my bare feet tucked under me. I'd tossed my stilettos across the loft. One had landed on the kitchen counter. The other slid under my bed.

Django's head was nuzzled in my lap. I tried to calm myself by petting him. I stroked his furry ears until his eyes rolled back, showing the whites.

"And on top of it all, you left me stranded," Dante said.

"I called a car to come get you. The LUX. The really nice one."

"That's not the point." He gave an exaggerated sigh. He stood looking around my place, trying to find fault. But I'd been keeping it spotless lately.

"Dante. I couldn't deal. I just couldn't."

"What's going on? You've never had this type of social anxiety or whatever it is." His voice was so gentle it brought tears to my eyes.

"It's not that."

He raised an eyebrow.

"It was him."

"Just because he's famous? That's absurd. You never cared about stuff like that before. Now, suddenly, when investors want to throw money at you, you are star struck."

"He's famous?"

"Hello? He's building the first apartment complex to orbit the moon."

"Oh crap. That guy?"

"That guy? Dante said rolling his eyes. "Wait...you really didn't know that?"

"Obviously not."

Django got up and headed for the door to the roof. He put one large paw on the lever and the door opened. The jingle of his dog tags and the soft thud of his bulk going up the stairs were the only sounds for a few seconds.

"I thought you just didn't recognize him. I thought as soon as I said his name you'd know exactly who he was."

"Wrong." I knew I was being a bitch. I reached for my bag and extracted my silver cigarette case. I stood and headed for the door to the roof. Dante followed me up.

I plopped onto a cushy chaise lounge and pulled a cashmere blanket up around me. The fog had rolled in and it was fucking freezing on the roof, but I didn't smoke indoors anymore.

Dante surprised me by grabbing one of my cigarettes and lighting it. I bit back a smart-ass comment.

"What's your problem, Gia?"

"I don't know." My voice was quiet. Now, in the safety of my own space, my behavior seemed ridiculous.

"I had a lot of explaining to do to our hosts."

I winced. "I'm sorry, Dante. I'm just a fuck up."

"Quit using that as an excuse to be a flake." His voice was hard. It was possibly the cruelest thing he'd ever said to me. Well, besides the time he said his husband's murder was my fault. Tears pricked my eyes.

"I'm sorry."

"You're lucky. He's agreed to give you another chance."

My eyes widened incredulously. Anger flared through me. "Give me another chance? Like I'm his bitch? Bullshit. I don't care if he can afford to live on the moon or around the moon or whatever. I don't need him or his money."

Dante was quiet for a few seconds.

Full-fledged alarm zipped through me.

"Do I? Dante? Do I? What are you saying?"

I heard him inhale. "I've been trying to tell you this. We were going to discuss it at the last board meeting you missed."

I shuddered and not from the cold.

"Discuss what? Am I broke?"

"Well, you aren't personally. But the corporation is foundering."

I stood up, startling Django. "That's impossible."

"The Detroit project? It hit some snags. Apparently, a crooked contractor has delayed progress. He is taking us to court over the work."

"Just pay him off."

"It's not that easy."

"Damn. I knew I should've gone out there to oversee the project instead of letting you convince me to go on some lame-ass cruise on which I was nearly murdered." My voice rose sharply. But I instantly regretted my words. "I'm sorry, Dante. I know you were just trying to help. To save me from myself. As usual."

Dante had arranged the cruise as a gift to try to help yank me out of my ongoing depression over my boyfriend, Bobby's, murder. He and Dante's new husband, Matt, had been shot when gunmen had stormed the wedding reception in Positano. The man behind it all had been trying to kill me. I made him pay. But taking his life hadn't been enough—the grief was still palatable every single damn day of our lives.

"Dante, are we really hurting? The business, I mean?"

"Well, we need a fast infusion of cash. Because of the stipulations in your father's will, I can't tap your personal funds for this. If Thornwell wants to throw his money at us, this is our best bet. He's agreed to meet with you Tuesday in his office, although, I must say, he's making an exception for you. Most Silicon Valley business is done at parties like the one last night."

"That's absurd." I remembered the man asking me if I liked it rough and the women in bondage gear. "Sex parties?"

"I don't know if that's what they are."

"That's the vibe I was getting." A fucking understatement. "Shit got all *Eyes Wide Shut* in there."

"I guess some people go off on their own at these parties and have sex. It's sort of a freewheeling deal in this crowd," he said.

"This crowd?"

"The powers of Silicon Valley don't play by the rules. They are always pushing boundaries, especially in the sex department," he said. "They're into lots of wife swapping and orgies, that kind of stuff."

I stood and paced my rooftop. The ubiquitous fog had settled revealing the glowing skyscrapers in the business district to the east. To the northwest, somewhere in the dark, was the Golden Gate bridge. I couldn't see it from my four-story building. But to the southeast, I could see the struts of the Bay Bridge.

But what I really liked to look at was my own neighborhood. The Tenderloin was filled with real people. Not like the insulated pocket of well-to-do in my old Russian Hill neighborhood.

The Tenderloin had a storied history of speakeasies, burlesque houses, jazz clubs, brothels, and crime. Though arguably more sophisticated, the crime, bars, strip clubs, and single-occupancy, pay-by-the-hour hotel rooms of today carried on their legacies and, in turn, had given rise to an entire small village of homeless people.

I knew many of them by name. One of them, Ethel, inspired me to start a new business within my father's company. I'd developed work-live housing to get people off the streets. Eligible homeless people could live in an apartment upstairs and work at one of the businesses at street level. They could stay there forever, or move on and open up a space for someone else. The street level of the building could contain up to a dozen storefronts. Anything ranging from acupuncture, to a gourmet market, to a café or bookstore. It all depended on the skills of the residents. One large area was open so people could have kiosks set up in an open market environment if they had more niche offerings.

That was the business Damien, and his partners at Sky Enterprises, wanted to invest in.

"So, they combine business with pleasure at their parties," I said.

He shrugged. "All I know is that they view themselves as different. They don't believe that societal norms and rules apply to them—that they're above them. And in some ways, they are right. Promise me you'll meet with him and hear what he has to say?"

I thought about everything Dante had said. In a way, this subculture fascinated me. I was all about laissez faire sex. And while the guy who grabbed me was lucky he got off with a kick to the balls, in his defense, he probably was expecting the bondage girls and had been acting appropriately.

"Promise me?" Dante repeated.

Dante only whipped out the "promise me" on rare, important occasions. He knew if I promised, it was a certainty.

I hesitated. It wasn't much to ask. Just hear the dude out? I remembered the irresistible pull I felt toward him and how I'd felt weak and powerless under his gaze. And that was from across a room. But that was a fluke. This would be different. It would be in an office building. During the day. It would be professional. I could handle being in the room with him for a half hour or so. It's not like we were going to strip down and fuck on his desk. We'd be talking business. Completely professional.

CHAPTER SEVEN-
Dream Come True

A s the clock struck midnight, everyone at the party was inebriated in some way. High or drunk or both. That was to be expected, of course. Sydney was convinced she was the only one in the room who was sober. Even if she hadn't wanted to be, she was still combating the effects of being drugged with a psychosomatic drug. She still saw flashes of lighting and heard thunder at odd moments.

She didn't want to exacerbate it with too much to drink.

Everybody at Joyful Justice wanted her to go on vacation and relax at the beach while doctors probed and prodded her and tried to "fix" her. But that was bullshit. Who had time for that?

When the mission to find Alaia came in to Joyful Justice, Sydney leaped on it. She was on the plane to France to meet Thornwell and Zimmer before anyone could object.

And Mulberry? The one who would object the most? The only person who could possibly even come close to convincing her to stay? He didn't even know who she was anymore. It was better to stay busy on a mission than let her mind spin off in that direction.

But it didn't stop her heart from leaping at every text or phone call, hoping it would be Mulberry on the other end, saying his memory had returned.

An image of Mulberry's bloody torn flesh on the battlefield flashed into her mind, unbidden. And the helpless feeling she'd had. At the time. And now. He'd lost so much blood he was lucky to have survived. But when doctors brought him out of his drug-induced coma, he only remembered the life he'd lived long ago, married to another woman.

It was like losing a piece of herself. Mulberry had been there from the beginning. He was the one there for her when she was still a New York City dog walker named Joy Humbolt who held her dying brother. He was the one who helped her become Sydney Rye. He knew her like no other. Without his memory of her and what they had shared, Sydney felt less solid, as if her life was an apparition that could float away.

Shaking off those memories and thoughts, Sydney scanned the room from a comfy chaise lounge, pretend sipping on the same tequila gimlet she'd been handed hours before. Every once in a while, she headed to the bar pretending to refresh it. The air was thick with marijuana smoke as people lit small pipes or joints and passed them around. Several small bowls of pills were in circulation as well.

As it grew later, the crowd at the party continued to thin. But it wasn't from people going home. If she hadn't been paying attention—or hadn't read Alaia's journal—Sydney might not have noticed the people escaping out a series of side doors. Sometimes there was a whispered conversation or a meaningful look, but for the most part, people just wandered off in pairs or groups, out one of the several doorways branching off the main room.

By three in the morning, only a hand full of the original twenty or so party goers remained in the main room. Much of Sydney's night had been spent fending off a couple wooing her for what she assumed was a threesome. It was exactly as Alaia's journal had described it.

The woman, pudgy and falling out of her top, kept looking at Sydney and licking her lips. The man was worse. He trailed his hand down Sydney's bare arm, and it took everything in her power not to thrust two fingers into his eye sockets.

Sydney hid her irritation and made her escape by saying she needed to check on Blue. She'd already checked on him twice, but they didn't need to know that.

Peeking through the window into the backyard now, she saw Blue's head resting on his paws and the other dog, a small, scruffy, bichon frise, snuggled up beside his chest, sleeping.

"Adorable, right?"

It was Zimmer.

"They seem to get along great. He's cute. What's his name?"

"Snuffles."

"You're kidding." She laughed.

"Nope. Damien was very adamant about the name."

She turned away from the window.

"Are you having a good time?" His eyebrows drew together in concern.

"You have a lovely home."

"Thank you. It's a dream come true."

The house was surrounded by a small forest. Gurgling fountains bubbled every few feet. Everywhere one looked was green. Birds sang, even in the dark.

"It's my little slice of nature."

"It's really peaceful. Serene."

She turned to face him. "Do you always do business at four a.m. at a private house with everyone high?"

He chuckled. "Well, Damien and I like to think we are reinventing the way business is done. We do it our own way and it applies to how we find new ventures, how we feel people out to see if they are good fits for a collaboration."

"Am I good fit?"

"I've done some research on your company, CyberForce. I think that providing private security with the high-tech devices you've invented would be a great partnership. It dovetails with our interests."

Sydney nodded. Dan had done a great job creating a shell company with a glossy website.

"You mentioned magnetic implants in hands that will act much like a chip does in an animal, but on a less invasive manner."

"We are also expanding into devices that monitor health." Sydney watched Zimmer carefully. Alaia Schwartz device was along those lines. She waited to see if he would react. But he only smiled.

"Tell me more."

"The subdermal devices implanted in the hands would monitor blood pressure and blood sugar levels and send the results by Bluetooth to medical facilities."

"Brilliant!" Zimmer said. "Do you have any devices we could test out?"

"The proprietary nature of the devices precludes me sharing them at this point in our conversation."

It was bullshit. How could he not see right through her nonsense?

"Fair enough. Well, we are most definitely interested in taking it to the next level."

Again, she nodded. The less she said, the better.

"Can I get you anything?" His voice had something in it. She looked up. He was solicitous, but there was something else in his manner she couldn't read. He seemed as if he were holding himself back. As if the coiled energy underneath his smooth, calm surface was barely contained. His eyes lingered on her lips. She swallowed. She didn't trust him.

He'd been gracious and a gentleman, but Sydney knew this didn't mean jack.

"Oh, there you are." It was the woman who had been sticking to her like a remora to a shark all night. Sydney hid her weariness and smiled. "Just checking on my dog."

"Karl wants to know if you want to take a dip in the hot tub."

"There are brand new swimsuits in the cabanas," Zimmer said. "If you don't mind, I'll join you."

The woman looked ecstatic. Sydney could only imagine what the woman was thinking.

Sydney begged off and said she needed to head home, allowing whatever hot tub debauchery was going to take place to occur without her. Before she left, Zimmer handed her a business card. "Here's my private number. Call me if you want to take it to the next level. We're in."

CHAPTER EIGHT-
Fake

M*ay 2001*
The high school hallway was deserted. The late bell had rung, and everyone had scrambled off to class. He waited in the meeting spot, a small alcove leading to an emergency exit. He stared at the graffiti on the wall.

A group of seniors spent lunch hour hunkered down in this hallway pretending to study, but really, they were probably discussing drug deals and girls they'd fucked.

He'd always watched the group with envy. Especially because Steve was part of the group. Steve had been his best friend in first and second grade before the jocks had commandeered him for football.

They'd quickly grown apart. Now, if they crossed paths in the hallways, Steve would jut his chin at him. He wasn't a dick. He just wasn't a friend anymore.

Same as Lila. She'd lived next door to him since they were babies. She'd always been nice to him in elementary school. He remembered one day when he had to go to the bathroom and Mrs. Kopenske wouldn't let him. He'd begged for a potty pass, but she told him he should've gone during lunch.

Lila stood and told the teacher that her parents had said it was always okay to ask to use the bathroom.

The crotchety old bitch hadn't listened to Lila and had sent her out into the hall.

He'd been extremely grateful to Lila. And in awe that she'd stood up to the teacher.

However, now that they were in high school, Lila rarely said hi to him or made eye contact.

That's why he was so surprised when she showed up at his house the previous day.

Her face was streaked with black makeup from crying. Her long dark hair tangled.

His mother had stood nearby, eavesdropping, until he glared at her, and she skulked back into the kitchen.

"If I don't turn this paper in tomorrow, I'll fail. My dad ..." here Lila let out a big gulping sob. "He'll ground me until summer. You're so smart. This would take me a week. I know it would only take you, like five minutes."

She thrust a handout at him. He glanced down. It was an essay he'd already written. And it had taken him longer than five minutes. He'd spent about two hours on it.

He glanced at this watch. It was already ten.

"Please?"

Her lower lip trembled so prettily. Her eyes had turned a brilliant green from crying. He nodded, and her face lit up with joy. She grabbed his arm, startling him.

"Thank you! Oh, my God. You've saved my life!"

They made arrangements to meet in the alcove after the late bell for first period.

Now, he waited in the alcove, head peeking out, not sure which direction she would come from.

Then the door to the girl's bathroom opened, and he saw her. She was adjusting her skirt and didn't notice him watching. She was so beautiful, it made his throat grow suddenly dry.

She looked up, catching him staring, maybe drooling, definitely acting stalkerish.

Her eyes narrowed, and a look of distaste flashed across her features. But it quickly disappeared. By the time she reached him and stepped into the alcove, she'd plastered a fake smile on her face, her lips curling up, her eyes remaining hard and cold.

But he'd seen how she looked at him. And he was humiliated. He'd been used.

He had been dumb enough to think she actually liked him. Not "like" liked him, but liked him as a person, as a friend. But now, in this alcove, as she kept glancing nervously over her shoulder, he knew that he repulsed her.

"Hurry," she hissed, holding out her hand.

He reached in his backpack, carefully extracting the stapled and typed essay.

Once it was in her hands, she shoved it into her own bag, wadding it up to make it fit. She turned to him, and her voice became saccharine sweet. "Thanks. You're a doll." She brushed past him, arching her body so they didn't make contact.

She paused at the entrance to the alcove. "I might have something for you next week too."

Her smile was fake. Her voice was fake. Everything about her was fake. He'd been a fool. Just because she'd been nice to him in elementary school did not make her a nice person. She was not a nice person. She was a cunt.

She hurried away before he answered. He watched her with narrowed eyes. Then he grabbed his crotch and thrust his hips toward her and spoke in a low voice. "I might have something for you next week, too. Something big and hard that will split you apart."

CHAPTER NINE-
A Regular Person

When I caught sight of the man sitting behind the large mahogany desk, I felt foolish for running away the other night. I still hadn't figured out what had gotten into me. A beam of sunlight fell across the papers scattered before him. The whole of San Francisco was on display behind him, visible in the floor-to-ceiling windows. His head was bowed, and his finger traced some words on a document before him. His lips moved as he read.

For a second, he reminded me of a little boy. There was a sweetness about his concentration. He froze, and I knew that he'd realized I was in the room.

When he lifted his eyes to meet mine, a genuine smile spread across his face.

"You came?"

He seemed so surprised. As if he were flattered.

Don't fall for it, Gia.

He stood, came around the side of his desk, and stuck out his hand.

"We haven't officially met. I'm Damien Thornwell."

"Gia Santella."

His handshake was firm. His eyes warm. He pointed at a chair in front of the desk.

"Please have a seat."

I gestured at the paperwork strewn over his desk. "Is this a bad time?"

He laughed, and his face lit up. His eyes crinkled as he did. "No, no, I was just killing time until our appointment."

For a split second, there was an uncomfortable silence. He looked like a nervous teenage boy. He swallowed, and his Adam's apple bobbed. Then his boyish awkwardness was gone, and he became the confident, imposing presence I'd seen at his house. But this time there was a competence and intelligence that had me intently leaning forward to listen.

"I've studied your new developments quite intensively over the past two months," he began. "The Miami project was impressive. The residents there have done a one eighty. One fellow I spoke to, Chad Nolan, told me how he'd been saving opioids up and was going to kill himself the night your staff members—you call them scouts?" He paused and looked at me.

"Yes, scouts."

He continued. "The night your scouts approached him, he'd made plans to end it all. At first, he brushed them off. But he said they treated him with such regard that he stopped and listened. When they told him they had handpicked him for a spot in the new development and were really hoping he could contribute his cooking skills, he thought he was dreaming."

"It must have been Liz and Doug."

Damien snapped his fingers. "Yes! Those were the names he mentioned. He said they were respectful, compassionate. Made him feel like a regular person."

"Good." I nodded. I didn't let just anyone become a scout. I usually interviewed and approved the candidates myself. I only hired the best of the best. They were the face of my company and they needed to be firm, empathetic, and savvy.

Ethel's Place was about treating everyone with respect no matter what their circumstances.

"When I met this guy, I would've never guessed he'd spent the last decade on the streets," Damien said. "He was full of life and enthusiasm, and man, oh man, could he cook. He whipped up a salmon mousse that melted in my mouth."

I smiled. I'd read about Nolan in the reports my Miami staff. That wasn't news. What *was* news was that a man as successful and busy as Damien Thornwell had taken the time to fly to Miami to see my project in action. I hated to admit it, but I was impressed.

Damien wanted to invest in Ethel's Place. A lot of money. An astonishing amount of money. I kept waiting to hear the catch.

Throughout the conversation, he was polite and professional—the perfect gentleman. He was gracious enough not to mention that I'd fled his party, and I again wondered what the hell had gotten into me that night.

"Do you think you might want to work with us?" He seemed nervous. I didn't get it.

"What do you get out of it?" I asked. "It's not like you need to make any more money."

He chuckled. "I've heard you were blunt. I see that was an understatement."

I looked away.

"Hey," he said. "It's refreshing. Trust me. I like it."

"You didn't answer my question."

He nodded, his smile disappearing. "Here's the thing. I have a reason that I want to be involved in this. It's personal, but if you need to know in order to move forward, I can explain."

A personal reason?

I bit my lip watching him. His body language screamed sincere. His posture was open and expansive. His eye contact was steady. His palms faced up and out on the desk. I raised an eyebrow.

"My father left us. He was an addict. He ended up dying homeless on the streets when I was ten."

When he finished, I waited a second before standing.

"Let's do this." I said.

He sprang to his feet. "Brilliant! Let me call in my partner, Richard Zimmer."

He grabbed the phone and spoke in a low voice. "Rich? Can you drop by my office? I want you to meet Ms. Santella. Thanks."

A few seconds later, the door opened. It was the jack ass who had gripped my arm the other night. My eyes narrowed. But he acted like he'd never seen me before.

He was wearing jeans and a gray T-shirt. *Prick thinks he's Zuckerberg or something.*

"Richard Zimmer. The pleasure is mine. I'm sure Damien has told you, we're both very excited to move forward and partner with you. I'll be handling the financial details. Damien is the creative. I'm the numbers guy. We can chat more later."

Like Damien, he oozed a winning combination of charisma and professionalism. Even in jeans. At least Damien wore a black button down dress shirt with his jeans and shoes shined to a high gloss.

I'd expected a couple of cocky assholes, but both men were deferential and charming as fuck—if, of course, you overlooked Rich Zimmer asking me if I liked it rough. For now, I'd give him a pass and chalk that up to him confusing me with the women who'd arrived after me. In the light of day, he was solicitous and professional.

The buzzer on Damien's desk startled me.

"Damien? Is Rich there with you?" A female voice.

"Yes, Sandy. We were just finishing up with Ms. Santella." He raised an eyebrow at me as he said it.

"Tell Rich his two o-clock is here. And by the way, your flight leaves the airport in fifteen minutes." She sounded irritated.

"I'm on my way."

There was no way he was making it to the airport in time. I felt the thumping vibration of a helicopter before I heard the actual sound.

He reached for my hand. "Deal?"

I nodded, and we shook. "We'll talk."

He grabbed a blazer and hit a switch. A panel opened revealing a staircase that probably led to the roof and the helipad. "Rich will walk you to the elevators."

Then he disappeared, the door closing behind him.

I followed Zimmer to the bank of elevators. He pressed the button and turned to me. His polite façade had vanished.

"We'll be in touch." As he said it, I caught something in his eyes—something that told me he remembered exactly who I was and that it had been my knee that clocked him in the junk at the party.

I stepped onto the elevator, and he watched me until the doors slid closed.

CHAPTER TEN-
Special Delivery

Sydney gripped the leather steering wheel, easily navigating the tight winding road from the Bay up into Oakland Hills. The sleek Porsche hugged the curves and accelerated powerfully with the slightest pressure from the ball of her foot. The top was down and her hair whipped around her. The morning air smelled like salt water and pine trees.

The G-Wagon in front of her was going even faster than she was and she fully expected to round a corner and find it had gone off the steep side of a cliff, and rolled into trees and houses below.

But Zimmer apparently knew this road well. Even though the larger, top-heavy vehicle drove faster, he handled the drive like a race car driver.

Sydney made sure to stay far enough back so they wouldn't recognize her in the rearview mirror, but figured she was safe since she'd used a car service last night to get to the party. As far as they knew, she was carless during her visit to the city.

She'd rented a Porsche so she'd fit in with the crowd she was running with.

At nearly the top of the hill, at a stop light, Zimmer's vehicle made a left. She followed as it turned off the main road into a heavily forested area.

Her Porsche was a little more obvious now. She slowed down, but still kept close enough to see the G Wagon's tail lights taking the corners in front of her. If they pulled over for some reason, she'd have some explaining to do.

When it was too late, she saw that the G Wagon had pulled into a wide circle driveway set back from the road. Keeping her head facing forward, she drove past. She pulled into a driveway a few houses up and turned around. There was a wide shoulder at that part of the road, so she parked and made her way on foot back to the circle drive.

Hearing voices as she got close to the driveway, she hid behind a tree.

After a few seconds, she found a gap between some trees and bushes where she could see the men perfectly. They knocked on the door of a long rambler set back from the street.

She dialed Dan. "Hey. Can you search an address?" She reeled off the number on the sign near her."

"Stand by."

A bush blocked her view of the person who opened the door. She could hear voices but couldn't make out what was being said. Both Zimmer and Thornwell returned and opened the trunk of the G Wagon.

What the fuck was going on?

The entire back was filled with boxes of diapers. Sydney frowned. Would they be delivering contraband pills or drugs in diaper boxes? Maybe. She'd heard of stranger methods than that.

But as she thought this, a nun in full habit stepped into view. Two other nuns followed. The men handed each woman a box of diapers and grabbed two each themselves. The group headed back toward the house. Sydney could see several faces peeking out of windows watching the whole thing.

"Dan?"

"It took a while to find out what it really is," he said. "It's registered to a shell company that is owned by Sky Enterprises."

Sydney waited.

"It's a safe house where abused women and their children can live indefinitely. A group of Catholic nuns run it."

"Fuck me."

"What? Are the nuns up to no good?" There was the hint of laughter in his voice.

"Just wasting my time, that's all," she said. "There's a missing woman and I'm watching two good Samaritans deliver fucking diapers."

"Good Samaritans named Damien Thornwell and Richard Zimmer?"

"Yes." She hung up.

Thornwell slammed the lid of the trunk just as Zimmer started the engine.

Sydney raced back to her Porsche. But by the time she was back in her car and headed down the road, the G Wagon was gone.

CHAPTER ELEVEN-
That Girl

January 2002

    His pathetic mother hovered in the doorway like the waste she was. He could smell the alcohol on her breath from across the room.

"That girl ..." she trailed off.

His irritation grew. "What about her?"

"The neighbor girl?"

"She's lived next door my entire life. Her name is Lila."

His mom looked a little confused and then smiled. "Oh, yes, Lila."

"I'm busy, spit it out."

He was on edge, every fiber of his being waiting. What would his mother say next? Dead. Or alive.

"She was found in that shack, you know the one up there." Her eyes rose as if he could see through the garage wall to the woods behind the house.

The shack that Lila and he had played in once when they were little. They'd played doctor. He'd unzipped his pants and she'd run away. Maybe that was when it had all gone wrong. But this time when he'd unzipped his pants, she hadn't been able to run. She'd been bound and gagged. He'd watched as her eyes grew wide with terror.

He was disgusted by her fear so he punched her in the face until she passed out. Then he took off his stocking cap mask and had his way with her. When he left, she hadn't been moving. It had been an entire day. Her parents had come over last night asking if his mother had seen her. He'd stayed in the dark doorway of his room, listening. After, his mother had come and knocked on his door. He'd stood on the other side, holding his breath. She tried the door, but the new lock held strong.

"They were asking about that girl? Lila. She never came home last night."

He remained silent.

"I didn't tell them she came here asking for you."

He closed his eyes and mouthed the word, "Fuck."

"I didn't tell them you did a load of laundry in the middle of the night. That had blood on it. I didn't tell them any of that."

After Lila had knocked on the door and his mother had turned her away, as she'd been told to do, he'd snuck out his window, donned a mask and knocked her out with a board on her way back to her house. He'd bound and gagged her and carried her over his shoulder up to the shack that was in the woods above their two homes.

Now, he waited to hear what the verdict would be. Dead. Or alive.

"Well, anyways," his mother said, "I wanted you to know that they found her. She's at the hospital right now. That poor girl."

He heard her softly crying as she walked away.

CHAPTER TWELVE-
Midnight Spin

I downshifted and revved the engine of my Ferrari, but the beige sedan in front of me didn't get the hint. The driver drove right by the wide gravel shoulder instead of pulling over and letting me pass. I wasn't in a particularly big hurry—I didn't have to be at Damien's place until two—but come on, this baby was built for speed. Throttling her back to fifty-five on a beautiful sunny Northern California day was a damn shame.

Inching my hood across the line, I saw a semi-truck heading my way. Resigned, I eased up on the gas pedal and looked over at Django, sitting ridiculously upright in my passenger seat, his long pink tongue hanging out, panting.

"What? Don't judge me. I'm nervous, okay?" I said. "What if you and his dog don't get along? Then what? You better be on your best behavior. No barking. No drooling. No humping."

Damien had texted me at three in the morning asking if Django and I could come to his house for lunch today. I waited until morning and said yes.

Finally, the sedan turned off.

When I stepped on the gas to pass another Sunday driver, Django whined. I didn't know about other dogs, but I knew mine sensed tension and could pick up my moods. When I was sad, which, let's face it, had been a majority of last year, he curled up beside me as close as he could get. When I was excited, he zipped around the loft, tail tucked between his legs, doing donuts and skidding into corners.

"It's okay, boy." After I safely pulled back into my own lane, I reached over and scratched his chin. "I won't do anything stupid. Not with you in the car, at least."

Besides, my car was only a year old and I planned on keeping it around for a while. I'd special ordered it after I smashed up my last Ferrari. I'd come back from Italy, blind with grief over the murder of my boyfriend, Bobby. I'd taken her for a midnight spin down the cliff-hugging curves of Highway One in Big Sur. The tree had come out of nowhere and I will swear on my mother's grave that I hadn't realized I had a death wish until the moment my airbag went off. It was only then that an overwhelming sense of relief enveloped me as my world faded into a soft, pillowy whiteness.

When I woke, the doctor told me I was lucky to be alive. The other side of the road was a sheer three-hundred-foot drop into the ocean.

I wasn't so sure about being "lucky," but I knew that I was so relieved to be alive I cried big fat sloppy tears. Guess I didn't *really* want to die.

When I made arrangements for a new car, I decided not to do red this time. Red wasn't turning out to be a lucky color for me. My last two red Ferrari's had ended up totaled. First one was demolished when my doorman went joyriding and the brakes went out and sent him and the car plunging over a cliff in the Marin headlands.

This time I went low-profile. I'd gone for the matte black Ferrari 812 Superfast. I'd also had them paint the wheels the same gunmetal black matte and remove all chrome. Anything shiny? Gone. I was low-profile as fuck in this 800-horsepower wet dream.

Well, as low profile as you could be in a 3,300-pound sports car that can hit a top speed of 211 miles per hour.

Despite the car's power, Django was not impressed. He curled up on the black leather passenger seat and put his chin on his paws, his eyelids fighting to stay open as he watched me. He was a bit neurotic.

For the past few weeks, he'd barely taken his eyes off me, following me around from room to room. It was my fault. I'd left him at home too often lately, running off to Mexico and then the Mediterranean.

I'd read that rescue dogs had abandonment issues, even if you weren't leaving them home while you traveled around the world like I'd been doing. But Django, a pit bull-lab mix was not your traditional rescue dog. I hadn't picked him up at a rescue organization, but I'd sure as hell rescued him. From some Tenderloin junkie who was kicking him in the head.

"Don't worry, Django. I'm not going anywhere again without you."

I hoped I was telling the truth.

"At least not soon."

I didn't want to lie. Even to the dog.

For the first time in a long while, I was filled with hope. And excitement.

I hadn't seen Damien since he'd stepped out of his office and onboard a helicopter a week earlier. I had to admit I'd been thinking about him ever since. At first I tried not to. But after speaking with him in his office, I'd been impressed. He was charismatic. Smart. And had a great smile and sense of humor.

But I wasn't quite ready to call today a date.

I now knew Silicon Valley techies did business deals during seemingly pleasurable activities. Like the sex party.

I leaned over and cranked up the volume on my speakers. Led Zeppelin was blaring and I was singing along at the top of my lungs. I smiled at Django and patted him on the head.

He just gave me a doleful look and settled back down to nap.

CHAPTER THIRTEEN-
Thunder & Lightning

Sydney headed back to the beach house to feed Blue.

When she arrived, there was a large black car with dark windows parked out front. She reached for the gun in her glove box and tucked it in her waistband. The other pistol was already in her bag, so she unzipped it as she warily stepped outside of the Porsche.

The driver's window rolled down.

It was Robert Maxim.

A flash of lightning raced across her peripheral vision and thunder roared in her ears. She shook off the hallucination. Then apprehension trickled down her spine. Was Maxim bringing news of something bad from Joyful Justice. What if something had happened to Mulberry? Or Dan? Or Anita?

But his slow smile relieved her of that fear at the same time it irritated her.

"I happened to be in the area and thought I'd see if you had time for dinner?"

Sydney looked at him incredulously. They were not friends.

They'd been through hell and back together—most recently on a mission in Syria, but they were not friends. Especially not friends who had dinner together.

He saw the look on her face and exhaled.

"I have some information you might find useful."

Sydney acknowledged his words with a nod and continued toward the door of her cottage, unlocking it and crouching to greet Blue.

Maxim was at her side. "May I?"

Sydney shrugged and he came inside.

An hour later, when Maxim left, Sydney laced up her running shoes and took Blue for a run on the beach. As she did, she thought about the information Maxim had given her. Sky Enterprises was working on a technology that could change the future of mankind. Maxim didn't have all the details but vague rumors on the shadowy dark web hinted at a mind-shattering possibility: That if Thornwell and Zimmer succeeded in obtaining funding for their creation, there would be no such thing as death.

Even Maxim agreed that it didn't make any sense and was most likely hyperbole, but he'd wanted her to know.

But all Sydney could think about during her run was the fucking injustice of something like this being invented after she'd lost the only person that mattered—her brother, James.

CHAPTER FOURTEEN-
Boom Box

O*ctober 2004*
    "Haven't you ever done this before?"

The naked girl in his dorm room bed watched him struggle with the condom.

He could feel his face grown warm at her words. Thank God, the only light in the room was from the candle near the bed. He was mostly in shadows over by the dresser where he'd retrieved an old condom package out of a drawer.

She was in his Physics class. She was actually quite smart. He'd been surprised she'd said yes when he offered to tutor her. But then again, this year, he was sort of a fucking rock star on his Berkeley campus. He'd developed a reputation as the guy with the best supply of feel good pills. He'd been dealing Ecstasy for the last six months after he hacked into his main competitor's computer and got the dude arrested by tipping police off on his next big drop.

As soon as he picked her up, she'd tugged down her mini skirt and grinned. "Hope this is an okay outfit for you to 'tutor' me in." She'd laughed and made quote marks around the word tutor.

He'd taken her to Thai food on Telegraph Avenue and then told her he had booze back in his dorm. She was game.

"I've got some X," he said.

"I don't do pills," she'd said.

Now that was a problem. She was supposed to be his next guinea pig. He'd planned to hand her a pill, passing it off as X. Now he'd have to dose her drink. The form of the love pills he'd developed were soluble. He'd perfected the combination now. It had taken three long years in the chem lab, working secretly while other students slept, but now he finally had the combination right—a potent cocktail of MDMA, oxytocin, SSRI's and a refined LSD mixed with pheromones that triggered serotonin levels that made people, well, fall in love. Or at least find him irresistible. Because right now all the pills contained *his* pheromones. Eventually, the pills would be custom made and people would have the pills tailor made with their own pheromones. It was his greatest invention yet.

It would solve problems such as loveless marriages and bolster arranged marriages. The best part of all was that the pill needed to be taken daily to remain effective. It was a built in, never-ending market. The demand for the pill would never go away.

He knew if he could patent the drug, it would surpass the monetary success he was having as an underground hacker and X dealer. Soon, he would be so rich that he'd have a dozen naked girls falling all over him at once, begging to be the one to put the condom on him.

HE'D PULLED THE ORANGE juice out of the mini frig and told her to relax on his bed while he made her a drink. But she wasn't good at listening. Instead, she put his Nirvana CD in his boom box and danced around him as he made the drink. Several times, he tried to reach for the small ceramic dish that held the love pills, but every time he started to do so, she was at his side.

Go fucking lay down on the bed like I told you.

But she wanted to gyrate against his ass instead. He eyed the pills and realized that he'd have to bring another girl home to be his guinea pig. This one wasn't cooperating. He needed to try it out on a girl soon. At least he'd get a fuck out of the deal.

The first girl he'd given it to last summer at Burning Man had gone into cardiac arrest.

Thank God, he'd been able to flee her tent and was miles away before her body was found the next morning.

After some heavy petting, the girl demanded he put on a condom. He had to get out of bed and search for one in his dresser, but was struggling to get it on.

The girl in his bed held up a hand in front of her and examined her fingernails. "You almost done?" she asked without looking his way.

"Yes," he said. "It's just this one is defective or something."

Why didn't she get up off her lazy ass and help!

"Oh." She rolled over and grabbed the pack of cigarettes off the nightstand. Lighting one using the flame of the candle, she glanced over at the dark corner where he stood with narrowed eyes. "I'm getting a little bored over here."

I'm going to fuck your brains out, bitch.

As she said this, the condom he'd been struggling to fit over his penis tore.

"Motherfucker." His voice was low. He closed his eyes and clenched his fists together at his sides. He could feel the rage building.

"That's it," the girl said, hopping out of bed and tugging on her dress. "I got a final tomorrow. We can try this another time." She grabbed her bag and brushed by him on the way to the door. He started to reach for her, but realized that the dozens of other students in this dorm hall might not be understanding of the noises they would hear if he forced her to stay.

The girl left, slamming the door behind her He stood there for a few seconds, filled with fury and humiliation.

He wanted to kill her. Murder her with his bare hands. But first he would fuck her.

This would never happen to Damien. Damien would know how to put on a condom. Damien wouldn't live in a stupid dorm room.

Damien would live in a place where screams could not be heard.

CHAPTER FIFTEEN-
Health Freak

Sultry jazz filtered out the open windows of Damien's house. From the front, the steel and glass structure looked like a fairly small rambler—a one story squat modern home, but I knew from my drive up to his house that the home terraced down the hillside another four levels overlooking the Pacific.

My dog and I stood in front of the gray steel door, my hand raised in mid-air.

Django looked up at me expectantly as if urging me to get it over with and knock. Although I'd felt comfortable around Damien in his office, something about him and his house sent tremors of nervousness through me. I told myself I was being foolish and knocked.

Damien opened the door with a wide grin. He leaned over and kissed both of my cheeks, sending a small ripple of desire through me as I got a whiff of his man scent and cologne. He wore faded jeans, a white linen shirt partly unbuttoned to reveal a slice of his chest, and white sneakers. His hair was smoothed back and he had a tiny bit of stubble on his cheeks and chin. This was Damien on his day off. I liked it.

Before saying a word, he crouched in front of Django and offered him the back of his hand to smell. Django sniffed it and then licked it.

"You're in," I said.

"Phew," he said, standing. "If a girl's dog doesn't like you, you're sunk."

"Sounds like you have some experience with that," I said, following him into the house.

"Not as much as you might think."

"Which one? With girls or with dogs that don't like you."

"Both."

He led me into the large living area and then paused.

"I'm going to go get Snuffles and have them meet here. More neutral territory than the backyard, I would think."

"Makes sense to me," I said, automatically, but then immediately thought, *who named their dog Snuffles?* I guess a grown man with enough self-confidence not to give a fuck what anybody else thought. I liked that.

I wandered over to the fireplace mantle to examine a few silver-framed photos. One was of Damien on a sail boat, tanned and smiling. Another was of him at the top of a mountain slope, his ski goggles pushed up on his head. A third was of him at the base of the Eiffel Tower. The fourth was of him and Richard Zimmer on a red carpet in Cannes, both dressed in tuxedos with women at their sides.

"Seems sort of vain to you?" His voice startled me.

I shrugged. What could I say? *Yes, you're too old for the selfie generation?*

I turned in time to see Django meet Snuffles. The blur of wagging tails reassured me.

"Looks like they're already friends," I said.

After a suitable amount of sniffing, Snuffles scurried off to grab a ragged chew toy and brought it to Django. With some small, playful growling, they each tugged on one end.

Damien handed me a glass. "Fresh orange juice. I just made it before you got here."

"Thanks."

He sprawled on a big white leather couch. I sat across from him, feeling awkward.

"I'm a little bit of a health freak," he said.

"What? Because you make fresh orange juice that makes you a tree hugger?"

"I don't really drink. I don't smoke weed. I drink a goddamn green smoothie every morning for breakfast, sleep eight hours a night, and workout for two hours a day."

I bit my tongue. He was pretty much the opposite of me.

But he misread my silence.

"So, about the pictures," he began.

I waited, but he didn't say anything.

"Uh, yeah?" I finally said. "Sure. What's the story there?"

"Those are the culmination—the proof—of years of visualization and dreaming."

"Go on," I said.

"When Rich and I were nerdy high school kids, none of the girls were interested in us. They all wanted to date the popular jocks."

"That's so cliché."

"Maybe. But true."

"We spent our entire senior year holed up in Richard's garage learning how to hack and code. At one point, I came across a book about what successful people do and discovered visualization. So, every morning I woke up and visualized *where* I was going to be when I was an adult and *how* I was going to be. I wrote detailed images of this life in a special notebook. Every day.

"I still do this. I keep a notebook that contains details of my life. It's not really a journal because it also has quotes I love and motivational passages. I have it with me at all times. In early modern Europe, they called these types of journals 'Commonplace Books.'"

"Cool," I said.

"For years, I wrote down and visualized different scenarios. One was snow skiing—tearing up the slopes. See, my family couldn't afford for me to learn to ski so it seemed something out of my reach for most of my life. The other was owning my own sailboat and sailing through the Panama Canal ..."

"And one was visiting the Eiffel Tower in Paris?"

He nodded.

"Did you really envision the red carpet at Cannes?"

"Hell, yes," he said, laughing. "In fact, I funded a friend's movie with the caveat that I could walk the red carpet at Cannes."

"With a gorgeous woman on your arm."

"Yes. Goes with the territory."

That made me stop. I had to ask.

"Why *are* you single, Mr. Damien Thornwell?"

He ran his finger around the rim of his empty juice glass. "Good question."

I finished my juice, eyeing him over the top of the glass.

"I could name a thousand reasons, but honestly, it probably boils down to me being too selfish."

I didn't respond. After a few seconds, he filled the silence.

"The crowd I run with, the people I do business with and socialize with—which ultimately are the same—we sort of feel like we make our own rules in this world."

I frowned. "I don't get it."

"Have you always been an heiress?"

His question sent prickles of annoyance through me. The word reminded me of dipshits who carried poodles under their arms.

"My parents didn't spoil me. I never really knew how much money they had until they died."

"Aha," he leaned back as if that explained everything. "So, we really aren't that different. It's just that to me, having this sort of money, and let's face it, power, is what I've always wanted. Call me a selfish bastard, but I made this happen and because of it, I do what I want, when I want, how I want. It's something I've earned."

That pinprick of distaste was there again. At the same time, his honesty was disarming and refreshing. Django came and sat at my feet and I scratched behind his ears. Snuffles hopped up on the couch by Damien. He drew the dog onto his lap and stroked his belly.

"In Silicon Valley, we don't really play by societal rules. We shun traditions. don't believe in societal norms. We believe in overturning paradigms."

"Like what?" I leaned forward.

"Well, you asked why I was still single, right?" He laughed. I didn't see what was funny about that. "Those of us who are married, well, let's just say, the marriage contract doesn't specify monogamy. Many of us believe that monogamy is an outdated notion to control us. We think marriage is an archaic institution formulated to keep people in line. A relic from Puritan times."

I thought of my parent's marriage. I thought of my mom's strong faith. These were two things I admired most about my family. I believed in monogamy, even if I didn't want to. I liked Damien all right and the chemistry between us was undeniable, but we were coming from two different planets.

Standing, I stretched. "We're just going to have to agree to disagree on that one. Where's that food you talked about? My stomach is grumbling."

He laughed. "I love a girl with appetites."

Appetites. Not appetite.

I shot him a look. He knew exactly what he was doing. It would be tough to resist him, but I was up to the challenge.

CHAPTER SIXTEEN-
Hindsight

There was something she was missing and Sydney wasn't sure what it was.

After her run on the beach, she showered and dressed and headed to Pacific Heights.

This time she knew to pull back the ivy and ring the doorbell at the mansion.

This time when Cyril opened the door, he seemed disheveled.

"I'm sorry I didn't call ahead," Sydney said. "I was in the area. I was hoping to look in Alaia's room again."

He left her and Blue alone again.

This time Sydney went straight to the stack of books near the bed.

Although it hadn't registered at the time, with hindsight, she'd realized that one of the spines was thin. It wasn't a real book. It was a day planner.

Now, she plucked the book out of the stack and flipped through it to the week Alaia disappeared.

The Brazil trip was on the calendar. And the day after she returned was the appointment that Sydney had been looking for.

Slipping the day planner into her own bag, she and Blue hopped in the Porsche and toward the city's financial district.

The high-powered criminal attorney wasn't in, but Sydney left her card with the secretary.

CHAPTER SEVENTEEN-
True Love Forever

D espite the rocky start, my day with Damien and our dogs had been one of the best days I'd had since Bobby's murder.

The conversation was easy and Damien was funny. I found myself laughing more than I had in months. It was relaxing to be around him. He was smart and cultured and sophisticated. Just my speed. We'd spent every night together after that for a week straight. We talked politics, cooking shows, indie films, and Impressionist art. But mostly we had mind-shattering sex.

A few times, the dark shadow of Bobby's memory had crossed my mind, but I'd pushed it back down. It was obvious that nobody could ever live up to Bobby. By dying, he'd achieved a state of perfection. I knew it. Might as well just accept it.

He'd be my true love forever.

But that didn't mean I was dead.

As much as I didn't want to admit it, Damien was growing on me. Besides his freewheeling views about monogamy, I was having a hard time finding anything wrong with him. He said he was selfish, but I also eavesdropped as he took two phone calls from people who apparently needed his help. In one, from Richard Zimmer, he argued with Zimmer to give someone a break about something. I couldn't hear Zimmer's side, but did hear his voice raise and saw the neck muscle in Damien's neck bulge as he told Zimmer to do as he said. No questions asked. The other call was about paying rent for someone else. He'd said, "Hopefully, she can get on her feet again. For now, just call off the sheriff's office. We'll pay the rent."

Once, outside my building, he'd spent an hour talking with a homeless veteran about politics. After a week spent together, I knew I'd have withdrawals when he took off on a ten-day trip overseas.

The day had ended at sunset, with him pleading off, saying he needed to get up at three to fly out of the country for ten days.

When we said goodbye, he'd leaned forward and for a second I thought he was going to kiss me, but instead he said in a somewhat nervous voice. "There's room on my plane for one more."

I had laughed. Of course, I had. But inside, I knew he was serious.

But the moment was gone.

"I want to see you when I get back." He said it as if I wouldn't dare refuse. So, I didn't.

"Okay."

I'd spent the entire time he was gone waiting for his texts like some lovesick idiot. The only healthy thing I did was double up on my Budo practice to keep my lustful hormones at bay.

And today, finally, was the day he was supposed to be back and I hadn't heard word one from him. And it was eleven in the morning.

I was making coffee when my phone buzzed. Damien had snapchatted me an image. I opened it. The words "Party at Zimmer's. Tonight, at seven. Dress sexy" were scrawled in hot pink script across a picture of a pool at night with candles floating on the water.

A party? I was disappointed that hadn't wanted to see me earlier and privately. That was bullshit.

Maybe I'd skip the party. To show that I wasn't used to being an afterthought. I wasn't one of the masses of women who shunned tradition and wanted to fuck him without strings attached. Not me, buddy. I make my own rules. Not you.

I was about to set my phone down when he snapped me again as if he sensed my reluctance. This time it was a picture of a brilliant white stretch of beach lapped by turquoise waves. The words said, "Come tonight. to receive exclusive details about our yearly soiree."

Huh. Intimate. Yearly soiree. What the fuck was that all about?

I was intrigued. So of course, I'd have to attend to find out more, but I'd make him work for my attention. I immediately headed toward the rack of clothes in one corner of my loft. If only Dante were here to help me pick out something suitable. I'd facetime him. Because this was one party where I wanted to look like a bad ass boss babe. Not Damien Thornwell's bitch.

CHAPTER EIGHTEEN–

Boom

Sydney eyed her phone. There was a snap from Damien Thornwell. It must've come when she and Blue were out walking on Ocean Beach.

For the past week, she'd dug up every scrap of information she could about Alaia and Sky Enterprises, and still hadn't found out what happened to the girl while she waited patiently for an invite to the next party. When her phone dinged from Thornwell, she didn't have to open it to know what it was. The invitation. Finally.

CHAPTER NINETEEN-
Success

May 2005
The girl lay by his side crying. She stared at the ceiling and the tears pooled at the corner of her eyes and then dripped slowly down her cheeks onto the bed sheets.

"I thought you liked me," she said, sounding stuffed up.

He was propped on one elbow looking down on her.

"I do like you. A lot." He traced a finger around her bare breast. She was incredible looking.

Maybe she'd want to fuck one more time before they had to get ready for graduation ceremonies.

"Then why are you breaking up with me?" the girl said.

He made a tsking sound. "Dasha. I'm not breaking up with you. We were never exclusive, remember? I've always been honest with you. We're both going to graduate and probably move across the country."

"That's not true. You're staying here. So am I."

"Dasha," he said, tenderly, wiping at her tears. "You'll get over me. There are going to be all sorts of guys who will want to date the hot nurse you're going to be."

"I only want you."

He could feel his chest inflate. "I know. I know."

Without realizing it, he glanced over at the small ceramic dish that sat on his dresser. He was going to be a fucking millionaire. The fucking pills worked like a goddamn charm. If the woman took them each and every day. He'd convinced Dasha they were birth control pills. She'd been too afraid if she went on the pill her conservative Hindu parents would find out about the doctor visit. He told her he'd take care of it.

She'd been his first success story.

He'd worked for the past two years to get the pills on the market, but the FDA had ultimately shot him down, saying it would not approve the drug with the risks involved: addiction, allergic reaction, even death.

Fine. It would be distributed as a black-market item. It would be all deep web and dark web sales. Now, to find the perfect business partner. He had just reached out to a hacker friend he'd joined forces with in high school. He knew he could trust the guy. And the friend's coding, hacker, and chemist skills nearly exceeded his own.

They'd go into business together and become the two most powerful men on the planet. Fuck the FDA.

CHAPTER TWENTY–
Sexy as Fuck

"Dress sexy has me stumped."

Dante laughed. "You always dress sexy."

"That is no help." I said, eying the stack of clothes on my bed. "Can't you come over and help me decide. This is important. I need to be sexy as fuck. I need to look like a boss."

From the sounds on the other end of the line, I knew this was an insane plea. It was Friday night at his new restaurant in Calistoga—some ninety minutes away if you were driving my Ferrari—and dinner preparation was already underway.

"Gia, you could wear a white sheet and you'd still be sexy as fuck."

"A sheet? I didn't say 'tacky as fuck" I said sexy as fuck. Please come down."

"Impossible."

My heart sunk.

"I have an idea. What time do you have to be there?"

"Seven."

He was quiet for a second and my heart stopped. Maybe he would come down.

"You'll arrive at seven-forty then," he said, and then he mumbled to himself. "Your outfit will arrive no later than seven. Have your makeup and everything else ready so all you have to do is throw on your clothes."

"Yes, maestro."

At seven my door buzzed. I raced down the four flights wearing a huge red kimono and bare feet. A man in a black tee-shirt and jeans stood outside the back of a livery car. He was holding a thick garment bag. He looked a little like an east coast gangster.

"Miz Santella?" And sounded like one. I liked him immediately.

"That's me," I said. He smiled and handed me the bundle. I tried to tip him, but he brushed it off. "Mr. Marino already took care of me. Have a nice night." He donned an imaginary hat and stepped back into the vehicle. I stood staring and then shrugged.

You never knew with Dante.

Upstairs I took the clothes out of the package and groaned. I punched Dante's number on my phone.

"I said sexy. As. Fuck. I said Boss Babe. Not Boss Man."

"Trust me."

I narrowed my eyes at the black mass spread out on my bed.

"It's Balenciaga," he said.

"Big whoop. So, let's get this straight—you want me to dress like all the *dudes* at the party?" Then it struck me. "Oh, fuck me! Is Damien gay? Or bi? Is that why you want me to dress like a man?"

"All the other women are going to be dressed—as you might say— 'tacky as fuck.' You want to stand out from them. The only thing you wear underneath are red silk panties. No bra. Nothing else."

I frowned. "How do you know I own red silk panties?"

"Oh, pleeeze, Gia. How long have we been friends?"

"Are you sure?" I eyed the black silk tuxedo warily.

"Yes. Oh ... and wear your lace-up stiletto Louboutin's. I had them hem the pants to fit those shoes perfectly."

"Of course, you did," I muttered.

"Have fun. I've got to oversee the execution of the hazelnut praline terrine at the mayor's table. Oh—and wear your hair down."

"Thanks, Dante," I said in a soft voice, but he'd already hung up.

STANDING IN FRONT OF the wall of mirrors in my loft, I smiled.

The suit fit like a wet dream. It hugged every curve of my body. My red polished toes peeked out from the hem of the silk pants. The lapel of the blazer dipped to my belly button, exposing bare flesh and the barest hint of cleavage on each side. A tiny swell. Such a small sliver, you might think you'd imagined it. Perfect.

I was rummaging through a shoe box of jewelry when I got a text from Dante. "Wear your dangling ruby earrings. Not the emerald ones."

I dropped the emerald earrings and reached for the rubies.

Dante was a goddamn virtuoso.

I glanced one last time in the mirror before walking out and nodded.

Boss Babe. Sexy. As. Fuck.

CHAPTER TWENTY-ONE–
Birds of a Feather

The security team that greeted Sydney and Blue at the door didn't mess around.

One man had a wand. "Please lift your arms."

Blue growled at him.

"Where's Jeeves?" Sydney said. "He's much more hospitable."

The two-blond hulking bodyguard-slash-musclemen were not amused.

The man held out his wand, his eyes lingering a little too long on her breasts while the other consulted the screen on his watch, scrolling through a tiny electronic list. His eyebrows were knit together in concentration. He obviously hadn't been hired for his spelling acumen.

"Just like it sounds," Sydney said to help him out. "S-Y-D-N-E-Y-R-Y-E."

"Got it." He acted embarrassed.

Blue growled when the man with the wand stepped closer. "I don't think he likes you," she said.

"Just doing my job."

Sydney walked past him with Blue flanking her. "Tell Mr. Zimmer and Mr. Thornwell that Blue doesn't like security wands. I'm sure they'll understand."

The long hall was lit by dripping wax candles in gargoyle sconces that gave the place a gothic feel. At the end of the hall, a rectangle of white light fell on the floor. As she grew closer, she could hear voices and laughter.

Pausing outside the door, Blue looked up at her expectantly.

She shifted so she could see inside and assess the situation before she committed.

The kitchen was as large as her whole rented beach house.

Half a dozen people huddled around a massive marble-topped island dead center in the room. An orange steel Bertazzoni stove dominated one side of the room.

Thornwell looked up. He had on a pink frilly apron covered in flour and a smudge of the white stuff on his nose. His eyes were crinkled with laughter. Zimmer was beside him, wearing a checked blue apron, his hands sticky with wet dough. He looked at her and held up his hands in surrender.

"I'd greet you, but trust me you don't want me to touch you right now," Zimmer said. The last part of his sentence was imbued with meaning. As if she were waiting to be touched by him. Sydney hid the disgust she felt and smiled.

"I hope it's okay I brought Blue again. He's awfully lonely back at my rented cottage."

The flicker of distaste that raced across Rich Zimmer's face was so subtle and brief, she thought she might have imagined it if she didn't already know what a creep he was. His face split into a wide grin. "You can put him in the back with Damien's dog. He loves it here."

Sydney smiled at Thornwell. "You brought your dog, too?"

"I always do. This is his home away from home. Snuffles suffers from some separation anxiety. Breaks my heart to see the look on his face when I have to leave."

Sydney smiled, but something about the way he said it was off. It was robotic. There didn't seem to be any real emotion behind it. She didn't quite trust Thornwell.

Zimmer jutted his chin at a door. "The backyard is through there."

For a second, Sydney hesitated. Her instinct was to tell him to fuck off, that Blue was staying by her side, but she had to play the game. At least for a little while.

"I know. Thanks."

Opening the door, she saw some steps leading to a massive pool area with a waterfall. The entire area was lit by Tiki lamps. Damien's dog, a little white scruffy thing, ran up wagging his little tail and crouching, ready to play. Blue looked at Sydney.

"You remember your friend, Snuffles," she said. "Have a good time. He's little, though. Don't hurt him."

Closing the door, she turned to the people gathered around the island. Everyone wore 1950s-style aprons. Flour and sugar and cinnamon and eggs were spread on the island.

"We're making dinner," Zimmer said. "Well, the roast is already in the oven. We're technically done with dinner and making dessert. Homemade cinnamon rolls. Want to help?"

Sydney shrugged and grabbed an apron from a big stack hanging on a nearby hook. It was weird that these ultra-rich people made their own dinner, but Alaia had mentioned in her journal that some of the sex parties went down like this so the host could excuse the household help for the night. It helped conceal the debauchery from strangers at the same time it helped the partygoers relax and build a bond before they got busy.

After Sydney walked over, Thornwell introduced the other women.

Cat had dimples and curves and didn't look old enough to drink. She wore thigh-high boots and a tight black leather miniskirt that was about six inches shorter than her apron. Maeve might have been old enough to drink. It was hard to tell what she was wearing, but whatever was under the apron was tight and white and several feet above her gold platform heels. The third woman, introduced as Zoe, was exotic looking with voluptuous lips, big hair, and caramel skin. She wore shorts that fit like men's underwear, a tight black top and bare feet. She might have been any age from nineteen to thirty. She didn't even bother glancing up when Sydney was introduced.

All of their eyes were slightly glazed. It had to be from more than the wine in the glasses sitting before them. That's when Sydney spotted a small ceramic dish on the island. Probably something interesting in there. Molly or Ecstasy. Something to lubricate the guests.

Sydney almost asked where the men were. Was this supposed to be Zimmer and Thornwell's own private harem?

But a few minutes later, three more men showed up. She recognized them as players in the tech world. Part of her last week had been spent memorizing the faces of all the big Silicon Valley players. These three were part of an elite group of up-and-coming tech rock stars. One was an entrepreneur. One a V.C. Another a founder.

They were introduced as Andy, Nick, and Tim.

At first, they seemed interchangeable because they were all dressed the same: jeans and black or gray tee-shirts. One guy had a black blazer over his tee, but they all had the same sort of haircut—longer bangs nearly hanging over one eye.

And wasn't it total bullshit that the invitation prodded women to dress up and yet the men all wore jeans?

That's when it struck Sydney—they were all emulating Thornwell and Zimmer. The hair. The jeans. The tee-shirts.

They'd just rolled out the cinnamon rolls and stuck it in one of the four stacked ovens, when one of the beefy security guys appeared in the doorway with a latecomer.

A woman with dark hair stood behind him. It was the woman at the party who had run away. *Well, now, things just got interesting*, Sydney thought.

The woman paused in the doorway. Sydney watched the woman stare at Thornwell, who hadn't noticed her arrival yet. There was something in the woman's eyes.

Up close, the woman's resemblance to Alaia Schwartz was even stronger. How odd.

Sydney watched her carefully. She'd get to know this woman. Maybe she knew something.

CHAPTER TWENTY–TWO-
Yin & Yang

The blonde woman was the only one not dressed like a stripper. She wore formfitting black pants and a loose, black silk blouse unbuttoned several buttons. Her nonchalance was sexy in itself. Her bob was tucked behind her ears. Her face unadorned except for a slick of lip gloss.

She exuded effortless chic.

Dante was right. Nothing was worse than trying too hard.

She caught me looking and met my gaze straight on with her unusual grey eyes and a slight curve of her mouth. I couldn't help but smile back.

There was something on her face. I stared until I realized what it was—her skin was scarred near her eye. Quickly, I looked away. But then fixed my eyes on her again. She took in my own scarred temple.

With a small movement, she raised her wine glass an inch and gave a slight nod. I lifted my chin in response.

As I watched, Damien leaned over and pulled back her blonde hair to say something. A green stab of jealousy ripped right through me. Was he fucking her? She laughed at whatever he said, but I noticed the smile didn't reach her eyes. She shot another glance my way and moved away from him.

Damien plucked the lid off a ceramic dish and held it before her. She shook her head with the slightest movement and he set it back down. He looked irritated. But then he noticed me watching.

"Gia!" he rushed over and swept me up in a hug. "How long have you been here?"

"Long enough." I watched his face, but his grin only grew wider.

He turned to the security guards. "Your services are no longer needed tonight."

The men bowed and ducked out.

"I missed you," Damien said in a low voice in my ear. "We just finished making dessert. Dinner is almost ready. Let me get you a glass of wine."

He turned to everyone else. "Go on in everyone and find your place setting. I'll be right there."

At his words, everyone shed their aprons, hanging them on hooks. Rich Zimmer didn't even look my way as he led the group out a different doorway. Dickhead.

I followed everyone in, standing uncertainly in the doorway.

After a few seconds, Damien appeared with a glass of wine and handed it to me.

Just then the blonde woman came over and said something in a low voice to him. He nodded and turned to me. "Why don't you join us? We're going to check on our dogs before we sit down."

Our dogs.

I followed them outside through some French doors. and was instantly jumped on by Damien's dog. I reached down and scratched his ears. Another big beautiful dog, nearly the size of a Great Dane, approached the blonde woman.

She leaned down, said something in his ear, and turned to me.

"I don't think we've met. I'm Sydney Rye."

"I'm Gia Santella." I wasn't sure whether to shake hands or not. She smiled.

"This is Blue."

"He's gorgeous." I leaned down to scratch him behind the ears.

We watched for a moment as Damien scooped up his own dog and was nuzzling it, burying his face in its fur and laughing as it pulled back and licked his jaw.

"I have a pit bull mix rescue at home," I said.

Damien must have heard me because he swore. "Damn it! I should've told you to bring Django!"

I looked at the two dogs giving each other playful nips. "He would have loved to hang with these two. For sure. He's dog deprived. I feel so guilty about it."

"Well, next time for sure," Damien said. "We better get inside before Rich gets his panties in a bundle."

I followed him through a door into the dining room.

It felt like we'd stepped into Dracula's castle.

The dining room had high ceilings, black curtains on one wall, and wall sconces with dripped red wax candles. A massive dark wood table covered in candelabras took up most of the room. Our group was already seated at one end of the huge table.

Damien looped his arms through both of ours so we were on each side of him. I felt like a fucking trophy girl at a Nascar starting line so I squirmed free. I noticed Sydney did the same.

Pulling back a chair, Damien gestured for me to sit on his right beside Rich Zimmer. He seated Sydney at his left.

I was introduced to everyone at the table. There were three other women, making a total of five. And four men. I wondered if this was why Damien had latched on to me *and* Sydney. I was getting a bad feeling about this.

But the conversation at dinner was casual and light-hearted, discussing the San Francisco Giants baseball team, the latest film from French modernist director Olivier Assayas, and how South Korea was trying to develop a robot soldier—a Terminator come to life.

"We pulled funding on that project," Zimmer said. "It was just too fucking scary."

Damien nodded. "I love A.I. and I definitely want to be at the forefront, but I refuse to finance anything that can be used in war."

I tried not to lean over and kiss him. The wine was going to my head.

Every time I finished my glass, it magically filled again. I mean, I knew Rich was refilling it with the bottles from the center of the table, but I never seemed to catch him doing it. The alcohol was making me feel sensual and a bit hazy. Suddenly, Damien had never seemed quite so cute. I couldn't stop laughing at everything he said. But then, again, neither could anybody else. He was the life of the party. I wondered if Rich minded playing second-fiddle to Damien. Every once in a while, I caught Rich watching Damien with an odd expression. I couldn't quite figure it out. It appeared to be a mixture of both disdain and admiration.

I noticed that Rich was very attentive to Sydney. Her glass never appeared empty, either, but I wasn't sure if that was because she was sipping the drink slowly or if Rich was keeping her well lubricated, as well.

CHAPTER TWENTY-THREE-
Full of Crap

Between Thornwell and Zimmer, the two men did a good job keeping Gia's wine glass filled, making Sydney worried for the woman. After all, the way Gia looked at him, it appeared she'd already drank The Damien Thornwell Kool-Aid.

The party had moved into the den. The entire floor was covered in fur throws and pillows. Dozens of gem-colored hanging Moroccan lamps reinforced the harem feel

Thornwell had Gia off in a corner, whispering something to her. His hand on her waist. He was isolating his prey. Zimmer's eyes flicked over to the couple. Sydney watched him scowl.

Well, *that* was interesting.

The exotic-looking woman with the British accent was the first one to plop onto the floor. She'd obviously been there before. She reached for a brightly painted ceramic dish with a lid and extracted a joint. Leaning over, she lit it with a candle. She peered into another container but then frowned.

"Where's the Molly, old chap?" she said, exhaling. "I'm ready for my taste."

Zimmer leaned down and kissed the woman long and hard on the lips. "Maybe I want you sober tonight, Zoe."

She snickered. "Hardly. Give it up, Richie."

He laughed and extracted a pill case with a mosaic lid from a shelf nearby. "Okay. Okay. Here's your taste."

Zoe grabbed the case and unearthed a small blue pill. She put it on her tongue and then lay back onto the cushions with a blissful smile.

Zimmer leaned over and pressed a button. Sensual Indian music poured out of hidden speakers. Zoe got up and languidly danced. The other two women joined her, caressing her body as she writhed in front of them.

Thornwell led Gia by the hand and drew her down onto a pile of fur pillows. He lit a joint and handed it to her without inhaling any of it himself.

Interesting, Sydney thought, wondering if Thornwell avoided drugs or if the joint was laced with something stronger he didn't want to ingest.

But Gia didn't hesitate to take a long pull off the joint before she passed it to the guy beside her.

Fuck, Sydney thought. Am I the only one here with any sense? She'd thought maybe she'd have an ally in Gia, but it wasn't turning out that way. Right now, it looked like she'd have to babysit her, too.

She flopped down in one corner and crossed her legs, reaching for a goblet of wine on a small wooden table near the floor. One of the men, Tim or something, sat down beside her, pushing back his floppy bangs and giving her a wide grin.

"Is this your first Rich party?"

She lied. "Is it obvious?"

He laughed. He had a sweet smile. "It's cool. They're a little different, but what's great is that it's all free will—you know. Nobody is pressured into anything."

"Pressured into what?" Sydney thought she might as well push the point.

"You know," the man said, ducking his head a little with embarrassment. "Taking Molly or having sex."

His cheeks bloomed red. Sydney thought it was cute.

"So, if I don't want to have sex or take drugs, it's cool."

He nodded fervently. "Oh, yeah."

"And you'll still like me in the morning?"

"Ha ha." He got up then. "Excuse me, I have to use the bathroom."

Sure, it was "cool." She knew as soon as he came back, he'd sit by one of the other women, someone who would say yes to Rich's party antics.

Sydney noticed Maeve watching her. The woman scooted closer and said in a low voice.

"He's full of crap, you know."

"Obviously."

"Here's the thing. You *can* say no. And then you're fucked later. My friend said no. Guess what? The promotion she'd been promised. Poof. Gone. She was, like, *persona non-grata*, at work after that. I mean, she still has a job and all that, but all that attention she'd been getting from her boss? It was bullshit. All he wanted was to have a threesome with her and his wife at a Rich party."

The woman had been whispering. But Zimmer and Thornwell hadn't missed a beat. Both men spoke in low voices and looked their way, although Sydney was fairly certain they couldn't hear what was being said.

Sydney's eyes narrowed. "And if you do? If you fuck them and take their drugs, then what?"

The woman stubbed out her joint. "You're fucked then, too. You might get the promotion. Get taken on some special trips and get special attention, maybe a shopping trip to Paris, but after a few months, you're back to nobody again."

"So, what's the play? What are you doing?" Sydney pretended to rummage in the ceramic bowl for a joint, watching Zimmer out of the corner of her eye, but she was listening carefully.

"I don't have one. I'm fucked if I do. And I'm fucked if I don't. I wish I'd never been told about these goddamn parties."

"Hey, quick question," Sydney said, glancing at Thornwell and Zimmer. Neither men were looking her way. "Do you know a woman named Alaia?"

The woman thought about it for a second, raising Sydney's hopes, but then frowned. "No. Not familiar at all."

The floppy-haired man came back and sat on the other side of the woman. She turned to him with a big smile, but not before leaning over to whisper to Sydney. "He seems the least harmless. Might as well get it over with."

The woman leaned over and placed her hand on the man's thigh.

What Sydney needed was access to that notebook that Alaia had mentioned in her text. Sydney had a feeling it held the key to everything. It was most likely in Rio, but it didn't hurt to look around here. She'd need an excuse to get up and snoop around.

Another man was staring boldly at Sydney. She smiled and looked away, playing coy. He would do.

CHAPTER TWENTY-FOUR-
Unstoppable

A *pril 2010*
Finally, after years spent in dark garages hacking security systems, writing code, and learning how to create the most potent MDMA drug in the world, they had made it.

They'd come up with a foolproof plan and the money was flowing like a river.

This was their year. By the end of the year, they'd both traded in their Corvettes for Porsches.

They'd sold their Russian Hill apartments for ridiculously priced homes in Atherton.

They donated their Brooks Brothers suits and flew to Paris to be outfitted in couture.

They'd been featured numerous times in Forbes Magazine.

It was what they'd dreamed about for years.

They were rich, powerful, and getting fucked as much as they wanted.

They were unstoppable.

CHAPTER TWENTY-FIVE-
Close Call

After a few minutes talking to the other man, Sydney approached Zimmer. He was lying sprawled on his back while both women, eyes glazed, stroked his jean-clad thighs and bare arms.

Sydney knelt down beside him. "I'm sorry to interrupt."

He smiled and grabbed her arm. She fought off the instinct to head-butt him or elbow him in the throat.

"Rich, I think I should check on Blue before I ..." she glanced back at the other man.

He laughed. "Your mutt is fine."

Sydney hoped he was too high to notice the fury she was sure had flashed across her face before she reigned it in.

"I just won't be able to relax until I check on him."

"What's your point?" Zimmer's voice had grown cold.

"I wanted to make sure it was okay with you." Again, she looked back at the man who waited expectantly.

Zimmer smiled. "Ah. Yes. All is good. Have fun. Breakfast is at nine."

Sydney stood without answering. She wouldn't be sticking around for breakfast. Now she had an excuse if Zimmer found her wandering around his house, she'd say she got lost looking for the door to the backyard.

As she forced a smile at the man waiting for her, she noticed Damien and the brunette slipping out a side door. For a second, Damien's eyes met hers and held them. His gaze raked her body, giving her goosebumps. She'd worry about him later.

IT WAS EASY TO SLIP the Roofie into the wine glass in the candlelit bedroom. She just turned her back to the man and poured him more wine. She handed him the glass but he waved it away. She'd have to try harder.

"I really dig the taste of red wine on a man's mouth and tongue."

That was all it took. He downed the glass and then threw it against the wall, roughly pulling her on top of him on the bed. In less than three seconds, she had repositioned herself so her knees had locked on-to the inside of his elbows and her forearm was pressed tightly across his neck. His eyes widened in surprise and he struggled to get free.

"Sorry. You're not my type."

Her choke hold made him pass out. By the time he regained consciousness, the Roofie should make his thinking fuzzy about what had happened. She hoped she hadn't given him too much, but she needed to make sure he was out for at least an hour. At the door, she glanced over and heard him breathing steadily. He'd live. Locking the door behind her, she slipped out and made her way to the north side of the house. She needed to find Zimmer's office and look at all his notebooks.

The office door was unlocked. Sydney's heart raced up into her throat as she stepped inside. More than anything she wished Blue were by her side, but he was her excuse if she got caught snooping around in this part of the house.

CHAPTER TWENTY-SIX-
Dangerous Liaisons

If I thought for a second I'd be able to resist Damien, I'd been fooling myself. I could keep my emotions locked up tightly, but the chemistry between us was off the charts.

Resistance was futile.

I knew what I was getting into. Pure, raw, casual sex with a powerful, charismatic man. Possibly the most charming and formidable man I'd ever met, in fact.

From the minute he greeted me in the brightly lit kitchen handing me a glass of wine, to the time he took my hand and guided me by the waist to a sumptuous guest bedroom, I was putty in his hands. I liked sex.

I especially liked sex with Damien.

He wasn't the best-looking guy around. He was fairly average looking. He had a trim body, but nothing spectacular. But it was the way he looked at me. It was the way he held himself, like a lion ready to pounce. And, ultimately, it ended up being all about how he worshipped every inch of my body in the bedroom.

After his comment about being selfish, I'd expected him to be a self-centered lover, but he was attentive and concentrated on my pleasure. Only when I'd exhausted myself with orgasms, did he let himself go.

Lying there in the candlelight from medieval iron lanterns, I turned to him.

"What's your secret, Caligula?"

He laughed, but then sobered. "Nobody has ever asked me that."

"They are just so satiated from fucking you, they assume that like everything else you touch, you are gifted, you have the golden Midas touch?"

"I guess." He turned on his side and put his head up on his hand. "But you see right through me."

I doubted that, but it made me flush with pleasure. "So fess up, Romeo. How did you get to be such an attentive lover? Tell me, was your first lover an older woman who schooled you in the ways of making love? A Mrs. Robinson?"

At my words a dark cloud seemed to pass over his features but quickly disappeared.

"You'll laugh if I tell you."

"I can't guarantee I won't."

He sighed and then pushed himself so he was propped up.

"Remember I told you that I didn't even have my first date until I was twenty because I was busy studying, working toward..." he threw out his arm. "All of this."

"This is Rich's house."

"You know what I mean?"

"Yes." My voice was quiet.

"I didn't want to be some bumbling idiot, groping a girl. Coming within two seconds of touching her. Shit like that. I wanted to be an expert."

"Mission fucking accomplished," I said, reaching for my glass of wine.

"So how did you become an expert?"

"This is the funny part."

"I'm ready."

"I took a class."

"A class? A class on fucking?"

"No. An online class on how to pleasure a woman. It was called something like how to give your woman a million orgasms or something."

"Oh."

"You're not laughing."

I shrugged. "Maybe it's because most men should take that class."

He smiled, then reached over and grabbed me and kissed my mouth, gently at first, then more urgently. He sat back and ran his fingers through his hair. He looked upset. For the first time since I'd met him.

"I didn't expect you to be like this," he said.

"I don't understand."

"Most heiresses are self-centered and spoiled and really shallow."

"Surprise."

He shook his head. "I don't do monogamy."

"So, you've said." I was annoyed. I never said I wanted to be monogamous.

"I like my life. I like my social circle. I never get bored."

"You don't owe me any explanation." I pulled the covers up to my chin. I was growing increasingly uncomfortable.

"I'm still playing catch up."

"Listen, Damien. You do your thing. I'll do mine. We can have great sex and leave it at that."

But he shook his head. "But I think I want more."

I stared at him blankly.

"But if ... just say if I had more of a relationship with you," he said. "I still could never be committed. I could never restrict myself to just one person. At least not sexually."

"Damien, I'm flattered, but I'm not ready for this conversation."

I stood and grabbed my clothes. He looked like I'd slapped him. I dressed and then leaned over and kissed him on the cheek.

"I need to check on Django."

He pressed his lips together and didn't answer.

I slipped out the door wondering why he looked so stunned.

CHAPTER TWENTY-SEVEN-
Soiree

Sydney searched everywhere in the office for that notebook. Worried about surveillance cameras, she'd worked in the dark, navigating by a small stream of light coming in from the lights outside the room at the pool. She'd looked nearly everywhere when she heard Zimmer calling her name right outside the office door. She raced for the room's French doors and slipped outside heading toward Blue at the other side of the pool. When Blue dog saw her, he raced over. She crouched and petted him and buried her face in his fur.

She sensed Zimmer before she saw him. He was standing in the open French doors leading to the office.

"There you are," he said, his clothes and hair disheveled. His gaze skipped over her body like pebbles on a pond.

"I was just telling Blue it was time for us to go."

Zimmer didn't move. Her heart pounded. Did he suspect her? Had she left something open in the office? Maybe he had cameras with night vision. She headed for the back gate.

"I think this leads up to the driveway, right?" She didn't wait for an answer. "I'm beat. My party date had too much to drink, so I'm just going to bail. Thank you for a lovely night. Talk soon?"

He stood still. She held her breath and paused at the metal gate while Thornwell's dog jumped on her legs.

"Thank you for coming, Sydney." He seemed angry, but as if he were holding it back. "By the way, I wanted you to meet everyone tonight in this intimate setting because I'm hosting all of you for our special annual soiree."

She paused.

"We leave for Brazil on Wednesday. Does that work with your schedule?"

"Only if I can bring my dog."

He nodded.

She left, relieved that even saying no to drugs and sex, she'd still garnered an invite to Rio. She was certain that is where she'd find all the answers to her questions.

CHAPTER TWENTY-EIGHT-
Sydney Rye

I'd just stepped into my loft when my phone dinged with a text from Damien.

Almost forgot. The soiree. We leave Wednesday for Brazil. Hope you can come.

Brazil. Hot beaches. Warm sun. Sex with Damien.

Sounded good. I typed. "I'm in."

Poor Django. As soon as I'd walked in, he'd run up to me and whined like he hadn't seen me for a year. And here I was promising to leave again.

But then my phone dinged again. "Bring Django. I'm bringing Snuffles. And Sydney Rye is bringing Blue."

Sydney Rye. The blonde he'd looked at so lustfully. Oh well. Not my problem.

Besides, it'd give Django doggy friends to play with during the trip.

Part of me knew I should pass. I had work to do for my father's company. My intention had been to only get to know Damien on a business level, to keep things professional. He was an investor for Christ's sake. When had he become the center of my social life?

When had taking a spontaneous trip to Brazil with him and his buddies become something that seemed normal? I wasn't a part of the

tech world. These men worked hard and played hard. They were determining the future for all sorts of industries around the world.

Me? I was a free spirit who only recently had cut back on my partying so I'd have more time and energy to devote to building mixed-use
developments for the down-and-out.

DJANGO BARKED IN THE middle of the night, waking me. It took
me a while to figure out that someone was knocking on my door.

I slid the bulletproof eyehole slot open and saw the blonde from
the party, Sydney Rye. Her dog was at her side. I'd forgotten how huge
he was. I opened the door.

Out of the corner of my eye I saw Django rise from his bed, hair
on end, nose arched forward, a low rumble of a growl in his throat. Her
wolf dog pivoted his head, honing in on Django. He didn't growl. The
dog had one blue eye and one brown. His eyes lifted to the woman,
waiting for her command.

"Django!" He turned around and curled up in a ball on his bed, but
placed his head on his paws watching our visitors.

"Come in," I said.

Kneeling down in front of them, I put the back of my hand out for
Blue to sniff. He looked up at Sydney. She nodded and he stepped forward, sniffing my hand and giving it a lick.

"Remember me?" I said, scratching under his chin. "You're a good
boy."

I backed up and headed for my galley kitchen. Sydney followed.
Her dog stuck tight to her side, tapping her thigh with his nose.

Django whined from the corner. Blue's head swiveled to see. I
looked up at the woman, and she smiled.

"That's Django." He wagged his tail as I said his name.

"Go play with your new friend," Sydney said.

Blue trotted over to Django who stood, wagging his tail so hard his whole body shook. They did their obligatory sniffing and then Django took charge, leading Blue over to the lever for the door to the roof.

He pushed the button, the door swung open and both dogs lumbered up the stairs.

Sydney laughed. "That's slick."

"Right?" I said. "I'll make some coffee."

THIRTY MINUTES LATER, we were settled in at my kitchen table. I'd finished my coffee and downed two shots of bourbon.

"I knew you wouldn't like what I had to say," Sydney said.

"You really think Damien knows that this shit is going on?"

She exhaled. "I can't imagine that he doesn't."

This woman had spent the last half hour blowing up my world.

According to her, Damien and Rich were behind some fucked up shit in the Silicon Valley tech world.

"Women are disappearing," she said. "It's been happening for several years. On average, one a year. The common thread? The women are all involved in tech and have some connection with Sky Enterprises. It looks like every one of them attended one of Thornwell or Zimmer's parties the week they disappeared. I'm looking into the most recent disappearance. Alaia Schwartz. She was last seen—or rather heard from—in Rio both of them."

"How do you know this?"

Sydney looked away for a minute and then said, "My company provides high-level security, so naturally we do deep investigations into any company we might work with. This came out during out digging. In the midst of our investigations, we came across a missing person's report and realized that Schwartz is the most recent woman who has disappeared."

"So, you've just taken on this investigation for the hell of it?" I didn't buy it.

Sydney laughed. "Of course not. The Schwartz family attorney has agreed to pay us handsomely for any information we might come up with about the woman. Let's just say the family could finance my company for the next ten years in the blink of an eye."

She was lying. But why?

"Why are you here? Why did you come to tell me?"

She handed me a picture of the girl. She was curvy with long, straight dark hair, full lips, and massive green eyes lined with kohl. She was holding a finger up to her lips in a suggestive pose. The nail polish was hot pink with a small setting of rhinestones that formed an "A."

"You say she was last seen with Damien and Rich? It's a pretty insular world, right? I mean there has to be more of a connection than just the company. I mean, the same people party together, right?"

Sydney didn't respond, just stared at me. She sat so still. Waiting. I squirmed under her gaze.

"Take another look at the picture," Sydney said.

I didn't understand. "What?"

Sydney steered me over to the mirror and held the picture up to my face. I stared at my reflection next to the photo for a second before I gasped.

"What the fuck?"

"She's your doppelganger."

"My eyes aren't green."

I didn't know what else to say. A woman was missing and she looked like me. Sydney was here because she thought I was in danger?

This new information and how it might be connected to Damien was disturbing, but I didn't sense danger. I really didn't know him or what he was capable of: A couple of dates and a few rolls in the sack didn't really provide insight into who he was deep inside. I'd always trusted my gut instinct on people. Right then it was useless, telling me nothing. But I remembered my first odd reaction to Damien—an instinct to run.

"Okay. So, Damien has a type. Is that a crime?" My voice was tight.

She stood and her dog was instantly at her side. "I understand how you feel. I had an obligation to tell you. To warn you. Especially when I saw your resemblance to the missing woman."

I stood, as well. Django ignored me, making me look bad. Why didn't I have a dog that read my every move as a command. We'd have to work on that. Sydney paused at the doorway to the loft.

That was where I was supposed to say thank you. But I couldn't get the words out. She stared at me, waiting for me to do something, say something.

Ultimately, all I could manage was a nod.

I followed her downstairs.

Before she stepped out onto the sidewalk, she paused.

"I think you should skip the Brazil trip."

I didn't answer. I shut the door and turned to head back upstairs.

CHAPTER TWENTY-NINE–
A Fatal Mistake

P*resent day*

Pouring the ice-cold vodka into the chilled tumbler took a precision his shaking hands did not have at that moment. A splash of the silky liquid spilled on his amethyst stone slab countertop. He swore and swiped at it before it could leave a mark. The interior designer had said it was sealed to prevent stains, but he didn't want to take any chances. That square foot of slab had cost as much as a new car. Well, a crappy new car that a janitor could afford. But still.

Downing the vodka would quell a tiny bit of the fury that had him seething and trembling, but he needed something more. It was his own fault.

Somewhere along the line he'd made a mistake. It was his own fault. The realization sent fury racing through his veins. He did not make mistakes. He was not allowed to make mistakes. He'd worked too hard to make a mistake of this magnitude. He downed the vodka in a single slug, trying to quell the seething and trembling brought on by his rage.

After downing the vodka, he spent an hour in his underground gym, piling the bar with more weight than he normally did. He worked at the punching bag furiously with both fists and feet until sweat poured down poured down his body and his muscles burned. Finally, he realized he had no choice. He dialed the private number and placed his order.

"This is going to cost you."

"I realize that. I'll transfer the funds immediately."

He held his breath, waiting for her acquiescence.

"This will be the last one."

"I understand," he said, and clicked the end button on his phone.

Fuck. He hated to burn that bridge, but he knew he could find another supplier. It's just that the more he veered from reliable, trusted sources, the more dangerous the game became.

He'd planned on holding off until Brazil. That way, his release would be utterly exquisite.

However, he hadn't counted on Sydney Rye scenting on him. He could see it in the way she looked at him. She knew something. She'd been snooping during the party.

He wasn't sure how much or what she knew, but he would be sure to find out once they were out of the country. He'd keep her close and keep an eye on her.

Until he found out just how much she knew, he would remain on edge, filled with tension and rage. But he had to hide it behind the sick, pitiful mask he had to wear for the benefit and comfort of others.

He had to find temporary relief. Even though it wouldn't be as rewarding as his plan to wait. After all, nothing was as sweet as nurturing and priming your prey before the final act.

But it was the only chance he had of taming his needs and the emotions thrashing through him, threatening to send him spiraling out of control. Because nothing else mattered more than maintaining control. He had to remain in control or he would lose everything he'd worked so hard for.

He reached into a drawer and withdrew a whip. Rhythmically slapping it against his thigh, he paced his lavish entry way, waiting for the doorbell to ring.

Finally, he heard the low purr of the livery car and a door slam. The woman's heels clicked clacked up the stairs.

He didn't wait for her to knock. He flung open the door.

She was so young. Almost too young for his taste. But womanly enough. She had thick dark hair, like he'd requested. Unlike many of her countrywomen, she was voluptuous. Maybe another client had paid for some work. Damien hated to think there were other clients. At least he had the satisfaction of knowing he'd be her last client.

Her fur coat was wide open and she wore a skin-tight rubber body-suit underneath—exactly as he specified. He was already hard.

"You're late," he said.

"Guess you punish me. I'm naughty girl."

He didn't answer. He'd prefer her English was better, but she would do. He smiled at her. The woman drew back slightly. He gestured for her to come inside.

She hesitated. Her eyes flickered back to the driveway, but the livery car was long gone.

Then looking at the whip by his side, she smiled and brushed by him into the house.

"You punish me good?" she said as she passed.

He watched her back for a second before he turned and closed the door, then paused to engage the security system.

"You have no idea."

CHAPTER THIRTY-
Not a babysitter

Sydney had done her job. Everything within her power. She'd warned Gia. What she really wanted to do was slap some sense into her. But, she couldn't save someone from themselves. Free will was real.

After seeing the woman was a doppelganger for Alaia, she had no choice but to warn her. Even if it tipped her hand. Gia thought she was investigating Alaia's disappearance for a nice paycheck. Fine. That would work for now.

Gia was stubborn and foolish, but she'd sealed her fate by throwing in with the likes of Zimmer and Thornwell. But Sydney liked Gia and knew she'd try to look out for her in Brazil.

Her instinct to protect the innocent was too strong.

CHAPTER THIRTY-ONE–
Blow out the Candles

I had a major buzz. The room at Café Katrina's was soft and hazy, just like how I felt. I'd slipped out back and smoked a joint, too, so I was feeling especially mellow.

Now, I slouched in the blue velvet booth and smiled, watching my friends.

They'd cleared some tables and were dancing under a disco ball.

We were celebrating Darling's birthday.

She was the first friend I made in San Francisco after moving from Monterey. I'd just been raped by a monster, and I was bitter and hated the world. At the time, I thought life couldn't get much worse.

Darling and I met during a protest after a cop had killed a young black man. We'd ended up in the back office of her salon afterward, drinking bourbon and plotting world domination.

For whatever reason, she'd trusted me immediately and I soon learned that while the salon was her passion, her real money came from her expertise at providing paperwork. The hard to get kind. Passports, driver's license, birth certificates, and so on.

But she vetted her customers thoroughly, and her clientele, was almost exclusively limited to people needing to escape hopeless or dangerous situations.

In my book, she was the queen of the Tenderloin—our neighborhood. We'd had to keep her birthday party invite only, or it would've overflowed the Bay Bridge into Oakland. Well, not really, but she had a lot of friends.

I loved her like an aunt. When my parents were murdered, she'd taken care of me, stuck with me through all my horrendous decisions. I could always count on her to have my back.

The same went for everyone in this room. I could count on them for anything. Looking at their faces, feeling buzzed from all the booze, I was overcome by such a feeling of gratefulness, I wanted to weep.

This room held the people I considered family.

There was Kato, my sensei. He perched on a bar stool, sipping ginger tea and laughing at something Darling was saying. They both watched Kato's wife, Susie, dance with George, Darling's new husband.

The former linebacker with the shiny bald head was a big teddy bear and not exactly nimble on his feet, but Susie grabbed his hands and guided him.

Polishing glassware behind the bar was Katrina. She was possibly the most beautiful woman in San Francisco and, now that Café Katrina was doing so well, one of the richest. She'd opened up locations in all the major metropolitan cities in the country.

My favorite tenant and neighbor, Thanh-Thanh, was there with her new man. They were dancing, too. It was too adorable for words.

Dante and his boyfriend Silas were trying breakdance moves. I wanted to warn Dante not to get hurt. Which was a joke, since he was nearly as fit as Kato.

At one point, Dante noticed me and whispered something to Silas before heading my way.

"I was going to invite James."

When would he get off this James kick. Didn't he know that James was too good for me? I would only hurt him?

Anyway, I hadn't thought about James for weeks. Not since I'd met Damien Thornwell.

I took a long slug of my bourbon.

"He's a cop," I said.

"Wouldn't hurt you to hang around a little law and order once in a while."

"Ha ha," I said. "You know he could lock me up for murder?"

"If you get married he can't testify against you."

That did it. I spit out my drink. It dribbled down my shirt.

"I'm dating Damien."

"Yes. The other 'D' in your life."

Darling had told me that for some reason the people closest to me would always have a "D" in their name. I believed her. Dante was my best friend. Darling was my mother figure. And Damien was my lover.

"Damien isn't really the type to settle down," Dante said, scooting into the booth beside me. His voice held pity.

"Well, neither am I. So, we're perfect for each other."

"I don't believe that."

I shrugged and rattled the ice in my empty glass, casting a look at Katrina behind the bar and hoping she'd catch my telepathic SOS—that I needed another drink and was trapped in the booth with my nosy best friend.

"When do you leave for Brazil?"

"O-five-hundred-hours, Captain."

"Cripes," Dante said, glancing at his watch. "You gonna sleep at all tonight?"

I shook my head, my hair swinging wildly. "Not if I can help it. I want to sleep on the plane."

"I thought you liked flying."

"I do. I just don't want to socialize on my flight. I don't want to have to be nice to a bunch of other yahoos on the plane, like this blonde chick who has a wolf sidekick."

"A wolf?"

"Looks like one."

"Cool."

I glared at Dante. Whose side was he on anyway? I didn't tell him what she suspected about Rich and Damien.

"Do you need me to help you pack?" Dante said with a big smile. "I can stop by your place on the way to our hotel?"

"Nah. I'm bringing a bunch of bikinis and cover ups. I don't plan to do much besides work on my tan," I said. "But thanks."

"I have a feeling there might be some fancy dinners involved if you are running with that crowd."

"Whatev. If Damien has a problem with my wardrobe, he can kiss my ass."

It was all bravado, though. I did care what he thought. I made a mental note to throw in a pair of Jimmy Choo's and a little black dress. Just in case.

What I didn't want to admit was that I was getting drunk to squash the slight apprehension about my trip to Brazil. It was that goddamn visit from Sydney Rye.

A new glass of bourbon magically appeared before me. I looked up and smiled. Silas. God bless him. He was so sweet. I took a big gulp and shook off the feeling of foreboding.

Despite what Sydney had said, I'd made my choice. I would stand by Damien. That meant going to Brazil. But at the last minute I decided to leave Django home. If something did go sideways or get weird, at least he'd be safe.

Dante got up to dance with Silas. He gave me a peck on the forehead before he left. "Don't forget to say goodbye before you ghost on me."

I laughed. But as soon as his back turned, I grew somber.

Despite my efforts to ignore Sydney's words, I couldn't help but mull them over. And wasn't she worried I would tell Damien about her suspicions? I wouldn't. But how did she know that? Did she say all that to scare me off because she wanted Damien for herself? It didn't fit. I mean, I didn't really know her. She *could* actually be that manipulative and evil, but I didn't really see it. For some reason, I knew she did have my best interests at heart. Even if she were wrong about Damien. I respected and admired her, but didn't quite trust her.

Just then my phone pinged. A text from James. I hadn't heard from him in months. It was if he had sensed we were talking about him.

"Got time for a drink Tuesday?"

My heart thudded in my throat. I'd told him a million times he'd be better off staying far away from me. And yet he kept coming back. Didn't he know I would destroy him and his life? He was a cop. I was a murderer. We were doomed from the get go.

I ignored the text. What could I say?

I frowned and took another gulp of my drink. When I set the glass down, the entire party yelled and gestured at me, reaching out hands for me to join them on the dance floor.

Shaking off my dread, I smiled and stood, dancing my way over to the people I would always call *mi famiglia*.

CHAPTER THIRTY-TWO–
Love Nest

S ydney's eyes were nearly closed, but she was acutely aware of everything that was going on aboard the tiny jet.

She clocked the movements of everyone. She was sure Blue, lying at her feet, was doing the same.

Gia hadn't brought Django and Thornwell hadn't brought Snuffles. He'd said something about how flying was torture for the little guy. Whatever. He'd told her before that he brought the dog everywhere because it had separation anxiety. Who knew what the truth was? Sydney suspected Thornwell just didn't want the added responsibility of caring for a dog on a pleasure trip.

Sydney wondered if the two had decided together not to bring their dogs? Fine. Blue didn't need any friends anyway. They had each other and that was enough.

But there was no way she was leaving Blue behind. He was not only her whole world, he was also her bodyguard. He had taken a bullet for her and he would protect her no matter what happened during this trip to Rio.

And things were getting a little weird already.

A few seconds ago, while she lay in her seat pretending to sleep, Thornwell had called her name. When she didn't answer, he'd called Gia's name. When there was no answer there, either, both men had stood and headed toward the rear of the plane. The men passed by her seat, leaving a faint trail of expensive cologne.

Sydney strained to hear what was being said, but the low rumble of the jet's engines turned the conversation behind her into intelligible murmuring. After a few moments, the men's voices grew audible as they walked slowly back to the front of the plane.

"I'm telling you, man, you have to sell it. Your little fucking love nest or fuck nest or whatever the fuck it is." It was Zimmer.

Sydney could hear the ire in his voice. The love nest? The *pied-à-terre*.

"I don't have to do anything." Thornwell's voice was ice cold fury, and his words came out methodical and evenly. "That's what I've worked for all these years—to do whatever the hell I want whenever I want. That's what we've both worked so hard for since we were teenagers. I don't have to do anything I don't want to."

"Bullshit," the word seemed wet coming out of Zimmer's mouth. "You have to get rid of it."

"It's not an issue."

"Clem."

Sydney caught her breath. Who was Clem?

Damien inhaled sharply.

Now they were in the aisle beside her.

Out of the corner of her nearly closed eyes, Sydney could see Thornwell ball his hands into fists. His knuckles were white and the back of his hands were bright red.

"I'll sell it before we return to the states," he said after a few seconds.

Zimmer sank into the seat beside her, mumbling. "Thank God."

But Thornwell remained in the aisle standing by their seats.

"Rich, don't ever fucking say that name again."

"Fine."

Then Thornwell's form disappeared toward the front of the jet.

Zimmer swore lightly under his breath. From beneath her lowered lashes, she watched him take out a bottle of vodka and pound two full glasses before he leaned back in his seat, closing his eyes.

Sydney couldn't wait for the plane to land. The overheard conversation had confirmed it. The *pied-à-terre* was in Rio. Now to find it. And find the notebook.

CHAPTER THIRTY-THREE–
Cherry Ice Cream Smile

I opened my eyes to see Damien leaning over my airplane seat, smiling and humming a Duran Duran song about Rio.

"You're going to want to see this."

The hum of the private jet's engines grew louder, and I could feel the negative G's as the plane banked steeply. We were beginning our descent into Rio de Janiero.

I pushed aside the huge cashmere blanket and raised my seat to an upright position, peering out the window at my side.

The view took my breath away.

On the left was a green mass, Corcovado Mountain, topped with the Christ the Redeemer statue. A low bank of fog clung to the far side of it, making it appear even more ethereal.

To the near right was an impressive skyline, the buildings glinting silver in the sunlight. And beyond them was the bay ringed with smaller green mountains.

"Unreal." I shook my head.

Damien smiled like he'd just opened the best Christmas present ever.

I matched his grin. Because that is exactly what it felt like.

Reaching for his hand, I said, "Thank you for waking me."

"Do you hang glide?"

I raised an eyebrow. "Sure. Why not?"

"I've scheduled a private hang gliding session for just the four of us at Corcovado Mountain," he said.

The rest of our group had flown on a different jet, but we would rendezvous at the airport and head to the beachfront villa from there.

A few seats away I spotted a blonde head and heard the impatient whine of the wolf dog. Her words of warning haunted me, but I pushed back the niggling thoughts in the back of my mind. I'd made my choice. I would believe in Damien until I had reason not to do so.

TWO GIANT, BLACK SUV'S waited at the private landing strip to take us to our beach house.

Damien told Sydney and her dog and Rich join us in the lead vehicle. I was glad. I liked her and her dog was amazing. Besides, I knew I'd have a hard time finding anything to talk about with the other two women who were runway models or something.

Rich and Damien remained outside the vehicle talking to the drivers.

After I settled into my seat, I whistled softly. The dog, Blue, looked up at his owner. She nodded and he came over and put his head in my lap. I shot a glance at Sydney and she smiled. "He likes you."

The smile on my face was genuine. I buried my fingers in the soft fur on his head and gently scratched behind his ears. I couldn't help myself and leaned down to give him a kiss on the top of his snout.

Sydney raised an eyebrow. "I can count at least a dozen people who would rather eat glass than put their face that close to Blue."

I nuzzled my cheek in his fur.

"I'm in love with your dog." Guilt flooded me as I remembered referring to Blue as her wolf sidekick. He was much more than that.

"He's my best friend. He took a bullet for me."

"Would love to hear that story."

She smiled, but didn't elaborate.

"I love Django," I said, "but he's sort of a big baby. Not sure about him taking a bullet for me. It's not his fault, though. His former crackhead owner probably abused him since he was a puppy."

Remembering this, I suddenly wished I'd killed that junkie instead of beat the shit out of him.

"There's a special place in hell for people who abuse innocents. Innocent animals. Innocent people."

Her words were loaded with meaning. I nodded. I couldn't argue. Even though I didn't believe that Damien was one of them, it didn't mean I disagreed with her statement.

I opened my mouth to explain, but the door opened.

Damien hopped back in with Rich behind him. Rich held a bottle of Champagne and four glasses.

I noticed how Sydney tensed when Rich plopped on the seat beside her. His eyes were hidden behind dark sunglasses.

We drove through the city of Rio, which was as cosmopolitan as New York City, teeming with massive skyscrapers bordered by turquoise oceans on one side and brushing up against green mini mountains on the other.

When we pulled up to the villa's gate, Damien leaned forward to speak to the driver. The driver said something into an intercom and the gate slid open. Before us was a three-story stucco home that stretched for a block.

The driveway was lined with thick palm trees and bushes that shielded us from the neighbors. I scanned both sides but only managed to catch a small glimpse of a terra cotta rooftop to my right. The villa was secluded on all three sides, but I knew from what Damien had told me that the backside was all beach and oceanfront.

Both vehicles parked in the large circle driveway.

I stretched when I got out, and Blue stretched beside me, making me laugh with delight.

While Damien and Rich helped the driver unload our luggage, I caught Sydney pouring her Champagne glass into a bush. When she saw me watching, she gave a long, slow wink.

"I'm a bourbon girl, myself," I said. But I thought about what I'd seen. She dumped the whole glass. I wish I'd done the same. I'd felt strange ever since I drank mine. It was a good feeling, though. I wasn't drunk, just buzzed and kind of horny, affectionate, and benevolent. Everyone was so sweet and here we are in fucking Rio de Janiero.

Blue went to Sydney's side, his nose tapping her thigh as we headed toward the stairs leading to the front door of the villa.

Inside, the villa was all terra cotta stone with high ceilings and arches. The main room opened up to a secluded courtyard filled with a fountain, a small swimming pool, and trees filled with tropical birds. Through the courtyard was another room that stretched the length of the back of the house. It was floor-to-ceiling windows overlooking the beach and the sea beyond. A small wall separated a stretch of sand between the house and the public beach. A few lawn chairs were set out facing the water.

"There is a high-tech security system between the wall and the house that alerts us if anyone who is not welcome tries to come close to the villa," Rich said, noticing where I was looking. "But all the locals already know this, and there are security signs on the other side of the wall alerting tourists."

Damien took my elbow. "I'll show you to your room. You can freshen up or take a nap or whatever. In a little bit, Rich and I are going to hit the waves for an hour or two. It's our ritual. The first thing we do when we land in Rio."

A small part of me was disappointed to hear "your room." But Damien had clearly pointed out he wasn't into monogamy or exclusivity and I'd agreed.

He'd been very attentive to me, but I'd also watched him dip his head to listen to the sexy English model speak. I think her name was

Zoe. Or Cat. Or maybe the other one was Zoe and she was Cat. I'd also seen him watching Sydney with narrowed eyes on more than one occasion.

I thought about Sydney and how beautiful and sensual she was. She wasn't interested in him, one bit. This was all business for her. That didn't mean he didn't have designs on her, though.

I didn't want Sydney to be right, but I also didn't want to be blinded by my feelings toward him. Every once in a while, his aggressiveness in sex bordered on something that frightened me. I could sense he was always holding back. That some other primal urge was kept barely under control. Maybe that's why he excited me so much. He was dangerous.

The upstairs of the villa held four massive bedrooms overlooking the beach.

My room contained a large bed with a white coverlet. A stereo system. A built-in bar. An en suite bathroom. And floor-to-ceiling windows overlooking the beach and water.

He nudged a closed door with his knee. "I'm right through there ... if you need me."

The way he looked at me made me turn and close and lock the door. His eyes never left mine as I pulled my dress over my head and made my way over to him.

Later, knocking on the door woke me.

"Damien? The waves have picked up." It was Rich.

Sitting up, he ran his hand through his hair and pushed back the covers. "I'm on it. Meet you out back in two."

I watched him walk to the adjoining door naked, waiting for him to say goodbye. But he slipped inside his own room and closed the door without a word.

Anger flared through me. Fuck him.

I threw back the covers and stepped into the shower.

CHAPTER THIRTY-FOUR–
In the Flesh

A s soon as she was alone in her room, Sydney unpacked her laptop. Blue settled in to the corner near the floor-to-ceiling window and exhaled loudly before closing his eyes.

Using a satellite connection that Dan set up for her, Sydney logged online and searched for any apartments Damien or Rich might own in Brazil

Nothing came up.

She dialed Dan.

"Hey."

"Hey."

"Did you search for any holdings Damien or Rich might have in Brazil."

"Not yet."

"That's where he killed her."

"You're sure she's dead?" Dan asked. There was something in his voice.

"Didn't we already talk about this?"

He sighed.

"There's somebody who wants to talk to you," he said. "I was going to call you tonight, but you might as well get it over with. Stand by."

"What? Who? What are you talking about?" But he'd set the phone down. She could hear him talking to someone else but couldn't make out what he was saying.

He got back on the line. "Okay. We're all set."

"What?"

"You're going to get a call through Skype. You're going to want to answer it. We'll talk when you're done."

As soon as he hung up, her Skype phone rang. Sydney answered and gaped at the man's face on her computer screen.

It was Alaia's father. Reginald Schwartz. Sitting by his indoor pool outside his daughter's cabana.

He wore white pants and a white blazer. He also had a cigar and a tumbler with a lime floating in it.

"You've got to be kidding?" Sydney said. "You're supposed to be dead. And yet there you are."

"In the flesh," he said.

"I don't have much time," Sydney said.

The man raised an eyebrow. "And I have even less."

Sydney left the odd comment hanging and waited for the man to speak. He took a puff of his cigar and then began with a loud sigh.

"I'll start by saying that my daughter has been a disappointment since the day she was born. It's not her fault. Her mother is ignorant and low class, a plebian. But beautiful. Provincial, but a looker. I could not help myself. I am a weak man. The flesh is weak, as they say."

"And you wonder why Alaia left home at sixteen."

Schwartz ignored her and continued.

"But there was always some potential there. My so-called death was a test for her, to see if she could tap into her Schwartz side. As I watched from the sidelines, I was pleasantly surprised to see that my daughter did inherit my business acumen and ambition. She just needed a little motivation. Her mobile health pod idea is brilliant."

Sydney felt her irritation rise.

"All this was a trick, a ruse to test your daughter? And then when went it went afoul, you had your attorney contact Joyful Justice?"

"I needed someone who could be discreet. And I'd read about you years ago on the deep web."

Sydney tried to keep her expression neutral, but she squirmed hearing that.

"I'm running out of time," he said.

"What, do you have some fancy gala in Paris where you need to be?"

"I am dying. That was not a lie. I just sped up my death date, so I could see how Alaia would act. So, far, I've been extremely pleased. But my plan was to come back from the dead and reward her for her ambition."

"Not to praise her and give her your unconditional love?"

His eyes narrowed.

"My fortune is proof of my love."

"Well, you might be too late." It was harsh, but Sydney didn't know how else to say it.

"I don't understand."

"As you know, your daughter was last seen in Rio and missed her flight back to America. I don't think she went rogue. I've since learned she had a meeting in San Francisco the following day with a high-powered criminal attorney. I think someone found out about that meeting and prevented her from being there."

To his credit, the man seemed devastated. His face grew ash white, and his lips pursed together so tightly they looked blue on the computer screen.

"I was afraid of that. Are you certain?"

"No. That's why I'm here in Rio."

"Who did it?"

"I'm here to find out."

"When you do, notify me. I want to handle it my own way."

Sydney exhaled loudly. "I'll let you know, but you might not get the chance to handle it your way. It might be out of your hands at this point."

Voices and footsteps alerted her that the group had returned from the beach.

"I have to go." She clicked off and switched to a screen showing costumes for the upcoming Carnival celebrations just as Thornwell entered the room.

Blue stood and growled, the hair on his back spiking.

Sydney held out her palm, and he settled back down, keeping an eye trained on Thornwell.

"It's okay, boy," Thornwell said, but he looked a little shaken. He walked over and leaned over Sydney's shoulder, his mouth near her ear, looking at her laptop screen. He smelled like a Pina Colada and sunshine with a thin veneer of male hormones. No wonder Gia couldn't see through him.

"This one would make you the bell of the ball, as they say." His voice was low. "Look here. It will be delivered tomorrow morning."

She stared straight ahead. Her finger pressed down, the cursor hovering over the buy button until slowly she clicked.

His hot breath was on her neck as he spoke. "Have you made a decision about our offer?"

Without turning her head or flinching, she answered.

"I appreciate this gorgeous trip. I really do. But the more I think about it, the less sure I am that my company and yours would mesh together."

"I don't understand."

She turned to face him now, making him draw back so they didn't collide.

"We are really pro women in my company. In fact, we only have a few men employees."

He smirked. "Your token men?"

Sydney shrugged. "Maybe something like that, but the point is, we are all about empowering women, which is something that is not really common in Silicon Valley. I was hopeful that your company was more enlightened than most ..."

She trailed off. Just to see what he would say. Whether he would defend himself.

"What changed your mind?" he said.

"I don't know. Maybe the parties. This trip. The drugs. The sex."

"You don't get it, do you?" His voice was filled with disdain. He stood and paced. "The girls attend the parties because they want to. Nobody requires it or forces them. I would still keep them as employees even if they didn't want to be part of the fun."

Sydney swallowed and paused a minute before answering. There were so many things wrong with those statements, she didn't even know where to begin. The "girls" didn't have a fucking choice despite what he claimed.

"If I don't get it, maybe you could explain it to me."

He helped himself to a drink from her bar.

He sipped half his drink before answering.

"We are reinventing the paradigms of society. Our work is reimagining and reshaping the culture. We don't need to follow outdated and old-fashioned rules about how to interact. About monogamy and inhibitions."

Sydney watched him. "So, you don't think any of the rules apply to you?" She kept her tone neutral.

He grinned widely. "Exactly."

"Okay."

"These women are embracing this new way. It's really the wave of the future. There will be no marriage or monogamy. Just you wait and see."

Sydney was happy to see he finally was using the word women instead of girls, but he was still so fucking far off the mark, she had to hide
her disbelief.

"You consider yourself ahead of your time. Ahead of the times in
general, then." It was a statement not a question.

"Bingo." He winked. "You get it after all don't you."

She didn't answer.

He stared at her for a second before speaking.

"I really hope you'll consider our offer. I think we could really be a
good partnership. I'll double the initial investment amount I offered."

She swallowed. He just put $40 million dollars on the table. For a
fake company, but still.

She didn't answer.

He slammed his glass down on her sidebar and turned toward the
door.

"We leave for dinner at the Hotel Copacabana at nine."

CHAPTER THIRTY-FIVE-
Eye-talian

Damien had called The Hotel Copacabana an "Art Deco treasure," but when we pulled up it looked like a really tall, really big white building across the street from the beach. The Copa was nice enough, but the way Damien had raved about it, I'd expected the Taj Mahal.

Before he and Rich bought the villa, he'd stay here during his visits to Rio.

"The Copa was designed by French architect Andre Gidare," he said. "This is where Orson Welles and Marlene Dietrich would stay when they came to Brazil."

I nodded as if that meant something to me.

"I was going to surprise all of you," he said, "but I can't wait to share the good news. I've been asked to emcee the Wizard Ball this year."

Raising an eyebrow, I half-smiled.

"It's the grand finale of Carnival. A very exclusive gathering here at the Copa. Once you emcee the event, you are put on a list and can never do so again. It's quite an honor."

"Cool."

He didn't seem convinced that I was suitably impressed so he went on. "Frank Sinatra was an emcee. Bill Clinton. Fidel Castro. Johnny Carson."

I smiled and nodded.

As we walked through the blasé lobby, I caught glimpses of hallways and giant rooms with Art Deco flair—ornate pillars, sleek marble floors, and brilliant chandeliers.

Once again, Damien was telling the group about how anyone who was anybody stayed here. That's when I got it. What mattered to him about the hotel wasn't the architecture—it was the prestige it carried.

Whatever.

But it made me wonder.

I hadn't thought of him as pretentious or shallow before. Then again, I didn't know him. Not really.

A hotel staff member led us into an enormous room with a massive, white grand piano holding center stage in the center of the marble floor. The staff member explained that the hall was used for weddings and other events and, that the following night, a famous Brazilian pianist's concert would be held there.

I felt right at home in my black cocktail dress that swirled around my ankles. Sydney wore a white maxi dress with small beading on it. All the men wore tuxedos. If it wasn't for the other two women's too tight and too short neon dresses, our party would've looked like we stepped out of the Roaring 20s.

Two women wearing gray-and-white bellhop uniforms complete with white gloves and little pillbox hats asked us to follow them. They directed us to red velvet chairs next to an Olympic-sized swimming pool reflecting the orange glow from the dimmed lighting inside the restaurant.

Because I'd been told we were dining at Copacabana Beach, I'd expected ocean views. But I wasn't going to complain. The pool, only a few feet away through open French doors, was lovely with floating candles.

Then, I saw the menu and realized we were seated at an Italian restaurant within the hotel.

For some reason this irritated me. I smiled and then quickly hid behind my menu, pretending to read it. I was ashamed of myself. I was acting like a prima donna. I hated women like that. I hated the way I felt. I was goddamn lucky to be sitting in a restaurant in fucking Rio de Janiero. Who the hell did I think I was being irritated that I had to eat Italian food.

But I was.

Maybe Dante was right and I was a fucking snob, but seriously, when in Brazil, I want to eat Brazilian food. Not Italian food.

Which I could've lived with until he made an announcement to the entire table:

"This is the best Italian food in all of Rio. I thought my little *eye-talian* princess would want something familiar."

I was pretty sure that lightning bolts were shooting from my eyes when I drew back from him. *Is that how he viewed me? Some fucking exotic bird to show off?*

Standing up so suddenly my chair tipped over I turned to him. "Fuck off." Grabbing my bag, I stormed toward the door. I was ready to fucking punch something.

I heard Damien calling after me and then heard some screams. I didn't bother to turn around to look.

On my way to the restrooms, I turned a corner and nearly mowed down a man in front of me.

"Fuck!" I drew back and then looked up.

It was Cameron Stone. The latest It boy, A-list celebrity movie star. Even I'd heard of him, which was saying something.

He looked down at me with a smirk. "You always swear like a truck driver?"

"Yep."

His smile grew wider. "I like that."

I shrugged and brushed past him. I was too angry to make polite conversation, even if the guy was gorgeous.

Looking in the mirror at my flushed cheeks in the powder room, I balled up my fists wishing there was something to hit. I did some deep breathing to calm down.

After a while, I felt a semblance of calm again. I'd go back and tell Damien off. Tell him he was completely fucking out of line and furthermore, had insulted me, and demand he apologize that instant. The fact that he didn't even realize this sent fury rising again.

Calm down, I told myself.

The door swung open. It was Sydney.

"He's an idiot," she said.

I didn't respond.

She watched me in the mirror.

"He's toxic. And probably deadly. You are infatuated at best and brainwashed at worst."

Fuck you, too. The words were on the tip of my tongue. But even though her statement sent a flurry of hate through me, I didn't want to make her an enemy. I respected her. I was curious about her. And I feared her. Because what if she was right?

She lifted an eyebrow as if she knew exactly what I wanted to say and why I wasn't saying it. Her features softened, and she reached out to touch my arm. I didn't draw away.

"I'm on your side. You need me, I'm there."

I nodded, acknowledging her words.

"By the way, you can go back to the table now. Damien won't be there for a while."

"Why's that?"

"Right when you left, an older woman fell in the pool. He jumped in to save her. He's upstairs getting changed into dry clothes the hotel is providing."

When I looked back up, she was gone. The bathroom door swung closed gently.

CHAPTER THIRTY-SIX-
Clem

Sydney woke early the next day. After a run on the beach with Blue, she was back in her room on her laptop searching before anyone else in the villa had stirred. Maybe Thornwell and Zimmer didn't own property in Brazil. Maybe one of them—or both of them—rented a room and took unsuspecting women there. But Alaia's text had said *pied-à-terre*. That seemed to imply ownership. Maybe not. Well, just to be safe, she'd try to find any records of the two of them or Sky Enterprises renting and owning other places in Brazil.

Sydney knew in her gut if she found that *pied-à-terre*, she'd find proof of what happened to Alaia.

She dialed Dan.

"Any luck?"

"I think I have something."

"I'm listening." Sydney sat up straighter.

"Do Zimmer or Thornwell have anyone working for them with the name Clem?"

Sydney froze.

"Why?"

"I found some property owned by a Celeste Industries in Brazil. The official owner is listed as Clem Smith, but it seems there is a convoluted connection to Sky Enterprises. It is vague and well hidden, but they are definitely connected through a shell company."

Clem was the name Zimmer mentioned on the plane.

"That's it, Dan!"

"I can't find an actual address, but I'm narrowing down the broker, who should have that information."

"Thanks, Dan.

"Sydney?"

"Yes."

"Be careful."

She hung up without answering.

THE PREVIOUS NIGHT Thornwell had announced that today would be a beach day for the group. Sydney changed into her black one piece and grabbed a cover-up, towel, and a faded Yankees baseball cap.

Their party filed out of the small gate at the back of the house around eleven that morning, lugging baskets with Turkish towels and sunscreen.

Blue watched with a sad look out the second-floor window of her room. She hated leaving him behind, but Zimmer had said the beach had a strict no dog policy.

Thornwell wore black bathing trunks. His chest was tan and fit, but not full of muscles. He wore dark sunglasses that hid his eyes as he held the gate open for Sydney.

He led them over to a spot roped off for beachgoers who had a reservation. The area contained lounge chairs with thick red cushions and umbrellas overhead. A man in a white shirt, black pants, and black vest greeted them. He had a white dish towel draped over his forearm.

"Mr. Thornwell," he said, nodding.

"I think we'll start off with a round of tequila gimlets this morning, Julio."

Thornwell looked at Sydney as he said it.

Big whoop, Sydney thought. *You remember what drink I like.*

Julio nodded and set off toward the hotel.

Thornwell threw his towel on a middle chair and nodded at Gia to take the one next to his. She looked annoyed and ignored him, putting her belongings on a chair at the other end.

She was apparently still pissed off at him. Instead of returning to the table last night, she'd disappeared. It turned out, she'd taken a cab back to the villa.

Sydney hoped that meant the bloom was off the rose, but it was hard to tell.

Without a word about the apparent slight, Thornwell scooped up his towel and put it next to Gia's.

Gia stripped off her white linen shirt and black shorts and headed toward the surf. She wore a tiny red bikini, and several men stopped to stare as she passed.

But their attention was short-lived. As Sydney looked around at all the bikini-clad bodies, she realized that, on this beach, the Brazilians looked like they'd all stepped out of a photo shoot for people with beautiful, fit, beach-ready bodies.

The Brazilians in general were stunning people. From the children playing in the sand to the grandparents resting under large umbrellas.

Thornwell stood watching Gia step into the ocean. The muscles in his jaw looked carved from stone. His pulse throbbed in his neck. His body was rigid and taut. Though she couldn't see his eyes behind his shades, Sydney could easily read his body language—he was angry.

She took it all in behind her own dark sunglasses.

Meanwhile, Zimmer, who was on her other side, kept yammering on about some A.I. technology he'd just invested in that he claimed would change medicine around the world. The company had invented pods that could do full body scans. The pods would be placed in shopping centers, gyms, even grocery stores.

Sydney had all but tuned him out, but as he described the technology, her attention snapped back. It was the same concept that Alaia had described in her journal.

She listened as Zimmer explained how it would work. The pod would scan and analyze body mass, blood pressure, bone mineral content, blood sugar levels, hydration levels, and so forth. The data compiled would be compared against statistical norms, and if there was a potential problem or risk, the person would be advised to contact their physician.

"Wow," Sydney said. "Who had this idea? Where did it come from?"

Zimmer shifted uncomfortably.

That's right, motherfucker. You snake.

"Um, my nephew. I, uh, helped him start the company last year."

"Really? Last year?"

It was Alaia's idea, and he'd stolen it."

Sydney realized that he'd probably killed her and passed off her idea as his own.

The vein on Zimmer's neck throbbed. "Uh, actually, maybe it was just a few months ago."

"Well, it sounds pretty cool." She reclined again. Let him think she wasn't on to him. Let him underestimate her.

Julio brought a round of drinks and Thornwell, still standing, took two glasses, downing them both and then heading off down the beach.

For a while, Sydney watched his back, but then he disappeared into the crowd.

GIA CAME BACK TO THE group smiling and tossing back her wet hair.

"The water feels amazing."

Sydney, who was on the other side of Gia, closed her eyes for a second, gearing herself up to be nice to Zimmer so she could get the information she needed.

Around one, after a brief nap and dip in the water, Sydney thought Zimmer had enough alcohol in him to be a little more forthcoming.

First, she asked what he looked for in an employee.

"We've got a shit ton of special tests. Two weeks' worth. Because the guy could be really talented, but we need to make sure dude can fit into the brogrammer culture.

Sydney couldn't hide her disgust. "Bro-grammer?"

"Yeah, you know like bro and programmer?"

It wasn't even worth bringing up the fact that some of the earliest programmers were women.

He was an idiot. Pure and simple. But that would make her job easier.

"What do you do to determine that?"

"One thing I like to do is a hot-tub meeting."

"Explain."

Sydney tried to hide the irritation in her voice.

"We hold our first interviews in the hot tub at my Lake Tahoe house. If a dude can sit in the hot tub for ten hours straight, then that proves he is Sky material."

"What exactly does it prove?" she asked, nonplussed.

The smirk on his face suggested he enjoyed her bewilderment. He didn't bother answering her question.

"We also take them to the casinos. If Damien is feeling really adventurous. He will fly them to Monte Carlo, and we'll play all night and fly back in the morning."

"Really?" Sydney tried to sound interested to keep him talking.

"We can tell if a guy can hang with us based on how he bets. If he doesn't go big—all in—he's probably not Sky material, you know. We don't have time for wimps in this business. It's high-risk, fast-moving. You gotta roll with the punches?"

He paused to take a sip of his drink and winked at Sydney over his glass. She smiled.

"We only bring on the best of the best. Because the coding we do, the inventions we create, the technology we launch, all of that is changing the future. We are actually fucking creating the future."

He sounded in awe of his own words.

A chill of pure fear raced down Sydney's spine. If these morons were the ones determining the future of the world, they all were fucked.

"Unicorn companies like mine don't have to follow the goddamn rules."

"What is a unicorn company?"

A smug smile crept across his face. "If you make more than a billion bucks a year, you are a unicorn company."

Sydney tried to plaster a suitably impressed look on her face.

Rich raised his hand to signal for more drinks and some nachos. "You know, with lots of cheese on them, okay man?"

When Julio walked away, probably internally rolling his eyes, Sydney tried to casually ask the question she really wanted answered.

"Do you guys have employees down here or is this just a vacation spot?"

Rich was shitfaced. He looked at her sideways.

"We just come down here to fuck around."

He closed his eyes. She was worried he'd fall asleep before she found out what she needed.

"Oh." She touched his elbow. "Is the villa the only place you guys own in Brazil?"

He sat up, his bloodshot eyes narrowing.

Fuck, Sydney thought. She'd said something wrong.

"Why?"

"Oh, I was just wondering what it would cost to own a place down here."

He examined her for a few seconds, his eyes watery and unfocused. Then he lay back down, closing his eyes.

Sydney held her breath waiting for him to answer the question.

"Nah. Only place we own."

CHAPTER THIRTY-SEVEN-
Purple Pills

I dipped my head under the waves, hoping it would cool off my anger. *How dare Damien treat me like a fucking piece of property. His "eye-talian" princess. Total fucking bullshit.*

He'd come to my room last night begging my forgiveness, but I'd told him I was going to bed, and slammed the door on him. This morning, he'd brought me breakfast in bed with roses and mimosas.

After two mimosas, I'd felt less hatred toward him. He'd fucked up, but he was remorseful. I told him he needed to give me some time to get over my anger.

"I'll give you as much time as you need," he said. "I was acting like a total jerk. I'm sorry, Gia."

Now, I swam parallel to the shore, feeling out of shape. I hadn't really done any Budo practice this week. If I didn't do some martial arts each day, I started to feel anxious and out of sorts. This swimming was doing a lot of good, but I needed something more.

I swam down toward one end of the beach where the crowds were thicker.

Damien had said earlier that as crowded as the beach would be that day, it was nothing compared to how crazy it would be during Carnival. It was one of the reasons he'd suggested we make it a beach day before all the festivities began.

I walked out of the surf, shielding my eyes to locate the hotel near our beach spot. I'd swam quite some ways away. The walk back would give me time to chill out even more. I wasn't sure why, but Damien's possessiveness had sent me over the edge.

That's when I spotted his familiar form in the crowd. His head was dipped, and he was speaking to a dark-haired beauty in a white bikini. She tossed her head and tried to jerk away, but he yanked her entire body toward his. He grabbed her by her hair and kissed her. Then he pushed her away, slapping her ass. She smiled back at him. As she turned, I gasped.

I stood still, astonished.

The woman looked like me.

Her hair was long and dark and in a similar style as mine. Her body shape, curvy. Same as me. It was hard to tell but it seemed like her features were similar, as well. But then she turned and hurried toward the parking lot, so I could no longer examine her features.

I thought about that woman, Alaia, and how we also looked similar and a chill ran down my spine despite the sun's heat.

Worried he would see me, I ducked my head and dipped into the crowd on the far side of where he was. My heart slammed in my chest; I could feel the blood surging harder and faster in my veins, hot with anger.

My entire body shook. The beach water trickled down my skin and twinkled in the hot Rio sun as I shuddered. It wasn't so much that he had kissed that woman. That actually didn't surprise me too much. He was a free agent. He'd made that clear. And right now I was so angry at him, I was glad that there was no commitment between us.

The part that disturbed me was that she looked like me.

And that fucking scared me. Because more than anything, I couldn't help but think: *What if Sydney is right?*

BY THREE EVERYBODY was suitably drunk and worn out from the sun.

Damien stood and stretched.

"Let's go home and take a nap before dinner," he said.

Which was ridiculous because that's what we'd been doing all day.

Back at the villa, I locked both my doors—the main one and the one adjoining Damien's room—before I hopped in to the shower.

But when I walked naked back into the bedroom, Damien was sitting on edge of my bed. His hair was wet, and he only wore a towel. Of course, he had a key. He handed me a drink. I downed it and he smiled and fixed me another.

Why the hell not?

He trailed a finger down my thigh and despite myself I wanted him. My anger at him had faded and was more irritation than anything. I wasn't crazy about him kissing another woman, but I'd agreed that we were not exclusive.

The alcohol he'd handed me had hit me hard. I felt languid and buzzed and not concerned about anything except his touch. As he kissed my bare flesh. I closed my eyes and let myself go.

Then, suddenly he was gone. I watched him slip through the door between our rooms. After a few seconds, he reappeared with a grin.

He held two small, purple pills with the name of his company, Sky, deeply embedded in them.

I raised an eyebrow.

"What are those?"

I didn't do pills. I didn't do crank. I didn't do heroin. The only thing I indulged in was booze and weed. I was old-fashioned that way.

He didn't meet my eyes as he spoke. "Something to enhance your pleasure. Save them for after dinner. I want to take you to a special place in town. Just me and you."

He did a damn good job not answering my question.

"What are they?"

"Molly." His voice indicated I was idiotic for not knowing, which made me even more determined to pass. "This is the purest Molly you will ever see in your life. We have our own manufacturer in Portland."

"Isn't Molly just plain old X, right? Ecstasy?"

He frowned and shook his head. "No. It's way better. And our Molly can't compare to anything else out there. It is the *crème de la crème.* The most refined form of the drug in the world. Pure as driven snow."

"I'm not really into street drugs," I said.

"It's going to be an FDA approved drug in the next year or two," he said. "Right now, the FDA has given it breakthrough therapy status. It's being used to help combat vets deal with PTSD. The results are astonishing. We've been backing some of the research and helping develop a form of it for Phase 3 trials."

"I don't have PTSD." Which was a fucking bold-faced lie, but whatever.

The truth was the last thing I needed was to have some feel-good drug in me distorting my thinking. I already felt out of sorts and fuzzy-brained lately.

He nuzzled my neck and then whispered into my ear. "Baby, I just want you to experience a pleasure you never have before. All your inhibitions will disappear. I promise you the sex will be mind blowing."

I was a little insulted.

"I don't know if you've noticed," I said, drawing back. "But I really don't have any inhibitions."

He laughed.

"True. But I want to share this with you. Please think about it."

Looking right into his eyes, I saw that he really meant it. He was pleading with me. Maybe I was a fool, but I couldn't help but think it was maybe because he thought I was special.

But then I brushed that thought away. Every woman who ever fell for a creep thought she was special to him.

I grabbed my bag and opened my door.

"I'm starved."

He didn't follow me out the door. I paused in the doorway and looked back.

"I'm going to go out with Rich after dinner," he said in a monotone voice. "Hit the town. Catch some live music. Do some male bonding."

It was a threat. If I didn't take the pills like he wanted, he was ditching me for the night? Fine. Fuck him.

He was still sitting on my bed. His face was expressionless.

Finally, he stood and said in a flat voice. "Remember, you were the one who wanted to be alone tonight."

Dinner was tense. I didn't sit by Damien and did my damnedest to ignore him. However, he made a point to personally keep my wine glass filled.

Sydney was closer to him, but kept shooting questioning looks my way. I wish we'd been sitting beside one another. I wanted to ask her more about her theory and see if she'd discovered anything else about Rich and Damien. The more time I spent away from him, as I had over the past day, the more I began to wonder if she was right.

After dinner, the two men said their goodbyes and took off in one of the SUVs.

I'd had too much sun at the beach and too much wine at dinner, so I was looking forward to a quiet night in my room and then an early bedtime.

Later, sometime in the night, I heard noises in Damien's room. He was home. I'd been having a dream about wild crazy sex with somebody—an unknown figure who had crept into my bed in the dark and was having his way with me. So when I woke, I was suddenly filled with desire for Damien. I'd slept naked and thought I'd go to him and slip into the sheets, surprising him. My irritation with him had waned and right then I just wanted some make-up sex.

But when I tried the adjoining door it was locked on his side. I was about to knock when I heard voices on the other side. Several voices. I put my ear to the door. I couldn't make out the words but then a few seconds later, I could make out the sounds. Loud sex sounds. Fuck him.

I stormed back to bed.

How had I ever got myself into this fucked-up situation and fucked-up relationship, if that's what it was?

The next morning, I heard more noises, giggling and whispers. But this time from the hall. I cracked my door and peeked out. Three people were leaving Damien's room. Two women and one man. Tim, Cat, & Zoe.

Damien's words came back to me: "Remember, you were the one who wanted to be alone tonight."

CHAPTER THIRTY-EIGHT-
Molding the Future

He glared at the morning sunlight filling his room. He paced his room naked. *Fuck.* Things were not going the way he had planned.

And that was unacceptable.

He hadn't worked as hard as he had only to NOT have everything go exactly the way he wanted.

She was a fool not to see what he was and what he had to offer. But she'd made her choice.

How dare her not choose him and his ways.

She would pay for that rash, stubborn decision.

If someone in his position of power and wealth couldn't get things to go his way, then things would have to change. Didn't they fucking know that his company controlled the future? What Sky invested in would dictate the way society was shaped. He and his colleagues were not just molding the future they were reshaping the world.

The love pill was just the beginning. Gia had provided the breakthrough. The dose had been perfected. The anger and paranoia others had experienced had been alleviated. Although, he really wanted to see what it was like when he combined the love pill with Molly, it wasn't absolutely necessary. He could dose her with it, but he knew she would notice right away. With the love pill, he could slip it into her drink and she would not realize she'd been dosed.

The experiment had been one-hundred percent successful. Now his buyer would be on board.

In exchange for the formula, Damien would receive enough money to launch an ungodly technology that would change life on earth forever.

He had developed the blueprint to create a brain-computer interface— an implantable device that provided a direct communication link from a person's brain to an external device.

The interface would have the capability of transferring a person's feelings, emotions, memories, and thoughts—essentially everything that made a person a person—onto a computer.

By allowing people to transfer their sentient beings to a computer or external device, the essence of a person could eventually be reinserted in a new, cloned body. People would live forever.

He would be God.

Now that he had perfected the love pill and would be able to afford to hire the brains he needed to create the device, he would not let anything or anyone stand in his way.

Yanking his phone from the charger, he punched in a number. He didn't wait for the person to say hello before he spoke.

"Take care of it. Make it look like an accident."

CHAPTER THIRTY-NINE-
The Shine

While I didn't particularly want to be around Damien, I did want to scuba dive. I'd done it once. A long time ago in Monterey. But this was Brazil. Damien had chartered two boats for our party, and we were going to spend the day diving.

When our cars dropped us off at the harbor, I took a minute to inhale the fresh sea breeze and stretch. We had a few minutes until the boat operator was ready. Damien was onboard the boat speaking to the crew and occasionally shooting glances our way. As I stretched, I noticed Sydney was doing the same, and we shared a grin.

I did a few Budo moves and she nodded at me in approval.

After we boarded and the boat started up, we all turned and faced the land we were leaving behind.

Far in the distance, the Christ the Redeemer statue looked down on Rio from the summit of Mount Corcovado.

"Tomorrow we hang glide up there," Damien said, coming over and wrapping an arm around my shoulder.

I fought the temptation to push him away.

One of the crew members, a teenager, passed out drinks—soda and beer— and plates of peeled shrimp and fruit and chocolate. Damien opened a bottle of wine near the front of the boat and handed me a glass.

As we left the small harbor and its sailboats, Damien pointed toward an area fronted by white sand and gleaming white skyscrapers. Copacabana and Ipanema beaches. I shielded my eyes to take in the spectacular views of Rio from the bay.

"That's where we will eat tonight," Damien said, pointing to the beaches and addressing the entire boat. "You can't come to Rio and not dine at least once in Ipanema."

He came over, handed me another drink, and wrapped his arm around me. I looked up at him and when he smiled at me, I forgot all about my irritation. When he leaned down and kissed me, I melted into his arm.

As we left the harbor, the wind and surf kicked up. Seagulls dipped in and out of the water. Our boat rocked on the choppy water and people reached for something to hold onto. Damien's forehead creased.

He walked up to the boat operator and said something.

Damien came back over. He pointed to a cluster of small boats like ours in front of the beaches. Our boat stopped as we waited for the second boat with the rest of our party.

"The captain wants to detour and drop anchor there instead of our original location. But I told him we didn't pay him to go where everyone else goes."

"Don't you think you should listen to what he has to say?"

Damien pulled back and looked at me. "You afraid? That's something I've never seen from you."

I grew rigid. "I'm not afraid." I said it in a low voice.

But when he turned away, I shivered as if somebody has stepped on my grave. My mother had called it "the shine." It was a premonition of danger. I looked around. We were in the middle of the ocean with a bunch of drunk men in a foreign country. A million bad things could happen.

The second boat, with the other half of our party came up beside us. The boat operators exchanged words. I didn't speak Portuguese, so

I couldn't understand what they said, but they both seemed annoyed and shot concerned looks at Damien.

Damien said something and the crew members reached over and held the two boats together so he could step into the other boat. Crew members began examining the equipment, looking at the tanks and lines and masks.

A man sat there with a grim look on his face. Unlike the rest of the crew, who wore shorts and T-shirts, he wore pants and a windbreaker. Damien leaned over and spoke to him. The man had sunglasses on and appeared to stare straight ahead.

Damien straightened and came back to the side of the boat. He was followed by the man in the windbreaker who climbed into our boat.

"This is Mario. He's the best diver and instructor in Brazil. I've hired him specially to instruct you newbies on diving. You will be in good hands. Rich, come over here with me."

Rich looked up from the beer he was sipping. As he made his way to the side, Rich stumbled a little. I could see irritation flicker across Damien's face, but it was quickly replaced by a grin.

"Never mind," Damien said when Rich got to him. "You stay put here and help Mario and the girls."

Damien turned to me. "I'm going to help out over here. One of the instructors called in sick this morning so I've offered to show Zoe and Cat how to dive. Nick and Tim are certified."

Zoe tossed her stunning mane of curls and stretched out her long dark legs and gave me a victorious smirk.

I grinned widely. It wasn't a fucking competition. She could have him. She seemed surprised by my smile and raised a well-manicured eyebrow before glancing at Cat.

Damien leaned over the small gap between the two boats, grabbed me by the waist, and gave me a kiss.

"Have fun."

Mario sat slouched in the corner of the boat. His silence was disconcerting.

The boats then started up again. We rounded the corner of a small island with a lighthouse before the captains turned off the boats and dropped anchor. Dark clouds had swooped in overhead, and the seas remained choppy.

"You first."

The man's voice startled me.

I turned. He was speaking to Sydney.

"Thanks, sailor," she said. "But I'm certified."

She turned and walked toward the front of the boat.

Mario got up so fast the entire boat shook. He stood behind Sydney as she inspected the equipment. He touched her elbow and said something pointing to a tank. She nodded and picked it up.

He turned and headed back my way. I noticed that Sydney waited until he wasn't looking and grabbed another tank.

She didn't trust him.

I narrowed my eyes. She probably had good reason.

Within a few moments, she had donned her gear and slipped over the side.

Her head bobbed in the water.

"See you."

And then she disappeared.

I turned toward the big bulk of Mario who was still watching the water where Sydney had disappeared. When he saw me looking at him, he said, "We will learn now."

"Okay. I know a little bit about it. I went once a long time ago."

When he finished giving me a refresher course, I was eager to get away from his morose manner and get in the water.

I strapped on my gear, put my mask and breathing apparatus in place, and tipped over the boat.

The weight of the gear made me sink into the silken water. It felt cool and glorious. As the light from the surface grew dim, I adjusted my regulator, but immediately realized something was wrong. My mouth filled with something granular. A tiny stream of air made it through, but I found myself gulping for a breath. Instead, I inhaled some of the gritty stuff. Oh my God. It was sand.

I reached behind me.

Although Mario had said nothing about it, a vague memory of my training in Monterey came back to me. The instructor had told me if something went wrong with my regulator, an "octopus—a spare regulator was always strapped on the back of the tank.

Although I clawed at my back, there was nothing there.

Then somebody slammed into me hard from behind, sending me reeling, knocking the regulator out of my mouth and causing me to gasp with shock. I got a glimpse of a man's back as I inhaled water. A fiery scorching pain filled my lungs. I panicked, thrashing in the water, turning in all directions. Seeing other divers close but too far away to reach. I kicked and flailed, but found myself sinking and choking, growing weak.

Then, from nowhere, Damien was beside me, eyes wide with horror. He ripped his regulator off and put it to my mouth. I tried to breathe in, but instead gagged. I spit out the regulator in time to vomit.

Damien grabbed my waist and propelled me up, but soon all was black.

I woke to see faces over me.

I was on the boat. I leaned over and vomited more. Choking and gasping.

Damien's face was closest. He was holding back my hair, his eyes bloodshot and wet. "Oh my God. Oh my God. She's awake. She's awake."

He cupped my head to his chest, and I could feel his heart racing against my ear.

"Hurry up!" He was screaming. "They can take the other boat. We need to get her to the hospital."

Then I felt the boat list and heard a thunk.

Damien swore. He set my head down gently, and then I heard him running to the other side of the boat.

"What the fuck do you think you are doing getting aboard this boat. I should leave you in the goddamn ocean to die, you stupid fuck. She almost died."

The man said something in Portuguese. I couldn't understand his words, but I got the tone. He was basically telling Damien to fuck off. I heard the sounds of a scuffle—grunting and the thud of fists connecting, and then a big splash. I was too weak to lift my head.

Damien was back at my side. He looked over his shoulder.

"Let the fucker swim to shore."

He sat me up and wrapped me in several blankets, wiping my face gently with a towel and smoothing back my hair. He kept leaning over and kissing my brow.

"Thank God you are okay. Thank God."

He held me close.

We were the only ones in the back of the boat as we raced back to the harbor.

Damien leaned down and whispered in my ear.

"I've never been so fucking afraid in my life."

He drew back and I saw tears in his eyes.

I was too tired to think about what his words meant. I was too exhausted and sick to care right then.

But I knew something had changed.

CHAPTER FORTY-
Drugged

Sydney couldn't convince the boat operator to return to the shore, so she stewed in anger and frustration as the other people in her party scuba dived and then got drunk.

Finally, when they reached the shore, she leaped out of the boat and hailed a cab, racing back to the villa.

She knew for sure now. At first, she hadn't been sure what she'd seen, but now she was certain. When Damien had poured Gia's wine, he'd slipped something into it. At first Sydney hadn't been sure, but the more she thought about it, she was sure that's what she had seen. He was drugging Gia. And probably had been this whole time.

Gia had to believe her now.

CHAPTER FORTY-ONE-
Out of Time

After the doctor had checked me out and said I'd be just fine, Damien had asked what I wanted to do. The others were still out on the boat diving. It seemed a little callous for them to continue their fun day, but hey, I was just some woman they barely knew.

"What I really want is to go to sleep."

He hugged me close and escorted me to the waiting SUV.

He'd been extremely attentive since my near drowning. It was sweet, but slightly odd, as well.

At the villa, he helped me undress and throw on a silk night gown.

He tucked me in, bringing the covers up to my chin.

"You going to be okay?"

I could barely keep my eyes open. I nodded.

"Here's your cell phone." He set it on the pillow beside me. "Call me if you need anything."

"Where are you going?"

He looked away, his teeth biting his lip.

"I gotta go let off some of this steam," he said. "If I don't, something is gonna blow."

He leaned over me, meeting my eyes. "I could kill that Mario. What a moron."

I grabbed his arm. "Damien. It was an accident."

"It wasn't."

The way he gritted the words, and the look in his eyes disturbed me. He was so convinced that Mario's negligence had nearly caused me to drown.

I touched his arm again. "Promise me you won't go after him?"

He smiled and seemed to relax a little. "Oh, I won't. Besides I've spoken to his boss. They'll handle it."

He left, saying he'd be back in time to escort me to dinner.

I was asleep before the door to my room closed.

But then Sydney Rye was at the side of my bed.

"He's drugging you."

I sat up. "What?"

"Damien is drugging you. I don't know why or what it is, but I saw him do it today on the boat."

"Why would he do that? And what kind of drug? I think I'd know if I was being drugged." But even as I said it, I wondered.

"It might not be something you feel. Look at you," she grabbed a handled mirror off my dresser and held it in front of my face. "Your pupils are dilated. Are you fucked up on something else? Something you took yourself?"

"No!"

"Then let me take you to a doctor and have your blood tested."

"I was just at the hospital."

"Did they draw blood?"

I scrunched my face trying to remember. It all seemed a little fuzzy. "No."

"Trust me on this one."

I stared at her. She was telling me the man who loved me was drugging me. It didn't make any sense.

"Years earlier I was dosed with Devil's Breath," she said. "Have you heard of it?"

I shook my head.

"It's a highly potent and devastating hallucinogen that puts you in a hypnotic state, makes you completely pliant. It allows people to lead you around like a fucking puppet. Frankly, I still have hallucinations from it."

She was so sincere. I frowned. "I'm sorry. That's really shitty, but I don't think it's the same. I don't feel drugged. I just feel like I've been drinking too much. I'll try to cut back."

Her eyes narrowed and she shook her head.

"Suit yourself." She slammed the door as she left.

Fuck. I didn't want her for an enemy. I respected and admired her and wished we could be friends, but she was wrong. She had to be.

Waking when the sun was setting, I felt oddly out of sorts. I didn't usually sleep that much during the day. But then again, I didn't usually almost drown.

I took a long shower and then dressed for dinner. Damien had said the restaurant in Ipanema offered South American food. I was hoping I'd have a bigger appetite later. Nearly drowning and vomiting up seawater and sand could effectively kill one's appetite.

I knocked on the adjoining door to Damien's room, but there was no answer. He must still be "letting off steam."

I dabbed on some perfume, strapped on some lace-up stiletto sandals, and headed downstairs.

I found Sydney drinking a beer and perusing her laptop on a couch in the large living room. Her dog reclined on the floor at her feet. He was so cute. He lazily wagged his tail when he saw me. I sat beside Sydney. I felt bad about our argument earlier. I really think she was just trying to help. Even if she was off base.

"Always working?" I said.

She took me in for a second. Before she answered the two other women walked into the room carrying fancy cocktails. The conversation was over.

CHAPTER FORTY-TWO-
First Kill

He paced the balcony of his *pied-à-terre* looking down on the busy street below. People were already preparing for the parade—flaunting skimpy costumes, carrying sloshing drinks down the street, and revealing slick-with-sweat flesh.

The sexually-charged atmosphere only heightened his lust. That's why he had purchased this *pied-à-terre*. At first. Because at that time, many years ago, he thought sex would be enough.

That was before his first kill.

Watching the life seep out of the someone's eyes made him feel invincible. He'd never felt more powerful in his life.

Bartering billion dollar deals, flying his own plane, even meeting the President of the United States—none of it could compare. If he were able to live orbiting the moon as he planned, maybe that would replicate the feeling of tremendous, all-encompassing power and the thrill of taking a life. Maybe not.

When he killed, he was God.

Usually he was able to keep his urges at bay. He allowed himself one a year. Here in Brazil. Far from the laws of his home country.

But recently that had changed. He realized that life was too short to restrict himself. And after he got away with the first one, he realized he was invincible.

However, to reward himself for all his hard work, he made sure to celebrate Carnival in his traditional way.

His caretaker didn't ask questions when, once a year, Damien asked him to drain the acid from the barrel he kept locked in his storage unit in the basement. He usually let the bodies decompose for about a year and then had the barrel drained right before he came back for the next year's Carnival.

He impatiently checked his watch. She would pay for being late.

The doorbell rang.

He kept his back to the door as continued looking out on the street from his balcony.

"Enter."

Her high-heels click-clacked across the terra cotta floor. He heard the swish of fabric and a small thump of her purse land on the ground. The next thing he knew she'd lifted the back of his shirt and pressed her bare breasts against his flesh.

"I'm sorry I'm late."

He glanced at his watch. "You are two minutes late."

"I was trying to get away, but the traffic ... Carnival, you know."

He whirled on her. "No, that is not acceptable."

She smiled and reached for him. He batted her hand away.

"That will mean two more minutes."

She cocked her head and raised an eyebrow.

"Two more minutes with you?"

He pressed his lips together. "Trust me. They will be the longest two minutes of your life."

A flicker of alarm raced across her face.

Good, he thought.

She's starting to understand.

He yanked her to him and kissed her so hard her teeth cut through her lip. He tasted blood. But she didn't struggle.

When he pulled back, there was still that slight hint of fear in her eyes.

"At the beach, you said you call me in next week. But you must really miss me."

"Plans changed. I was saving you for last."

Looking up at him, she examined his face. She didn't like what she saw there because her eyes flicked toward the door.

Too late for that.

"I wanted to have you after she was gone because you remind me of her."

"Of who?" She scooted a little toward the door.

He laughed. She thought it would be that easy to escape.

He continued without answering her. "But as I said, my plans have changed. I realized something incredible and unexpected—I love her."

Suddenly, he laughed. "I wanted to make her love me. But now I love her."

At those words, she seemed to relax. She looked up at him smiling. "Why you want me if you love her?"

"I need release."

"Oh, she won't before marriage? I have many clients, maybe Catholic, whose women won't before you know."

He yanked her hair so her face tilted up at his.

"Don't talk about your other clients."

Her eyes were wild. She no longer bothered hiding her terrified glances toward the door. He ran his hand down her hair, tangling his fingers in the long curls.

"I love her. I don't want to kill her anymore."

The woman erupted in nervous laughter.

"Kill? You so mad at her right now you feel that way, but if you love her, you will go over it. Of course, you don't really mean kill."

She examined his face.

He turned his full focus on her and grabbed her by the chin. Before she realized it, he stuck the needle into her neck. He had her hands bound and mouth gagged in seconds. It would take another few minutes for the drug to kick in fully.

She would be awake. She would be aware. But she would be trapped within her own body. Unable to speak or move.

Yanking back the comforter, he revealed the plastic-lined bed.

He laid her down and leaned over her so he could see the horror in her eyes as he spoke.

"That's exactly what I mean. Kill."

CHAPTER FORTY-THREE-
Welcome to Silicon Valley

Sydney was convinced that Damien was drugging me, but I'd looked into his eyes and seen the horror, the fear, and the love, when he had talked about my near drowning. It was hard to reconcile that with someone who wanted to harm me.

But as night drew near, I wondered why I hadn't heard from him. If he was so worried about me, you'd think at least he'd call.

And then, when it was nearly time to leave for dinner, Rich knocked and said that Damien had called *him*.

And that we'd meet Damien at the Ipanema restaurant.

I curbed my jealousy. It wasn't really my business how Damien spent his afternoon.

We'd established the ground rules from the beginning—an open relationship.

It was what I'd wanted, as well.

But I had to admit that at times I doubted my resolve.

Sometimes when he was sleeping peacefully beside me after lovemaking I envisioned that this was our life. It didn't have to involve marriage, but a small part of me wanted the security of a monogamous relationship.

He was waiting when our car pulled up to the restaurant and he rushed to the door, opening it, pulling me out by my hand and scooping me into his arms. He buried his face in my hair and inhaled loudly. "I missed you." He breathed the words into my ear in a hot rush.

I laughed. "I saw you a few hours ago."

"You look amazing," he said. "How do you feel?"

He drew back and examined my face.

"Back up to speed," I said.

That's when I noticed his hair was wet. He'd recently showered. I dismissed a flicker of jealousy. He'd shower after a workout, as well, right? Again, it was truly none of my business.

He turned to greet Sydney who was wearing a white, off-the-shoulder dress. She looked spectacular. And as if she hadn't even tried. Which, come to think of it, she probably hadn't.

We entered the restaurant and found our private dining room.

The walls were painted a deep green and the massive table and chairs were a faded turquoise. The whole place had an underwater vibe. Wall-sized windows overlooked the beach. The room was lit by candles in wall sconces.

I wasn't a jealous person, but when Damien sat Sydney near him and me by Rich, I felt a stab of envy. And insecurity.

But then again, I remembered the look in his eyes after he'd saved me today.

The people he'd fucked the previous night—and maybe this afternoon—were no competition. Not really.

But Sydney? She was another story. She was gorgeous and sexy and most importantly, smart. Damien liked smart.

I thought about our conversation earlier. Could she be right? My thinking was a little fuzzy. I didn't want to think. I just wanted to feel. I downed my glass of wine and poured another.

Sydney didn't notice. I felt guilty remembering I'd told her I'd try cutting back. I wouldn't. Drinking and smoking weed was my usual shitty way of not dealing. And without the opportunity to train at the dojo, I had few other releases right then.

I'd concentrate on enjoying authentic Brazilian food and the company around me.

When the waiter brought a seafood stew he called *Moqueca*, I knew I'd died and gone to heaven.

The first bite of creamy shrimp, coconut milk, and lime-deliciousness was orgasmic. I closed my eyes savoring the first spoonful, letting the flavors roll around my tongue.

I opened my eyes in time to see Zoe, the stunning English model, make a face and push her soup bowl toward the middle of the table.

The guy to my right was cute and engaging so I focused my attention on him instead of worrying about what Damien was doing. His name was Tim, and he was some big-time founder. He'd started a company that created a simple DNA blood test that could predict the odds of people developing certain high-risk cancers. The company was about to go public on the stock exchange, and he was poised to become the next Elon Musk. Or Damien Thornwell.

I'd noticed that Rich and Damien surrounded themselves with up-and-coming men and gorgeous women.

I turned to the woman on my other side. Her name was Cat.

"Tell me about your job again?"

"It's waiting on the men." She said it matter-of-factly and took another slug of her frothy drink.

"Is that what you want to do?"

"Hell, no," she said. "Why do you think I'm here?"

I shrugged. "A free vacation?"

"No. I'm here because I'm going to ask Rich for a promotion."

"To what?"

"Fucking CFO, baby. I have a masters in accounting and ten years of being a CFO for a bank."

"Nice." I raised my glass to her, but then grew somber. "Do you think you have to come here and fuck people to get that promotion."

"Duh," she said staring straight ahead.

"That's pretty fucked up."

"Welcome to Silicon Valley, bitches." She raised her wine glass in a toast to the room.

"Everyone is like this?"

"You're damned if you do and damned if you don't," she said. She was starting to slur her words. "If you sleep with them, they may not hire you or promote you. If you don't—same."

I nodded. "I've heard a little about that."

"Believe it or not. Rich and Damien are probably the most decent game in town."

"Huh." A waiter brought out some platters. One contained what looked like a grilled Octopus that had its head chopped off. It was surrounded by perfectly roasted potatoes and sprinkled with chopped scallions.

"Madame, *polvo na chapa*." The waiter announced with a flourish.

"Ugh. I think I'm going to vomit," Zoe said from across the table as she eyed the platter.

I reached for the serving spoon.

"Listen, I don't think we should talk about this anymore." Cat shot a glance at Rich who was eyeballing her.

Without looking her way, I said quietly, "I've got my own company. It's not tech. But it really could use a woman with your expertise. Why don't you look me up if you don't get what you want from these guys?"

Cat grabbed her bag and excused herself. She didn't respond to my offer.

I turned to the guy another chair down. Nick. He'd been talking to Zoe, but she was now leaning in and laughing at something Rich was saying.

He spoke about his start-up company with such assurance, I did a double take.

"How old are you anyway?" I asked.

"Twenty-seven."

"You're shitting me?" I said. I was nursing my fourth drink, and I knew the swear words were going to fly. I didn't care at that point.

He smiled. "You just say whatever you want, don't you?"

"Fuck yeah," I said and held my glass up so the waiter would bring me another. I was feeling no pain.

"And you like your booze?"

I examined him over the rim of my glass for a second before I said, not dropping my gaze. "I like all my vices."

A red flush crept up his neck.

He quickly regained his composure though, saying. "I guess you and Damien are a good match, then?"

I was startled into speechlessness. By a few parts of that sentence.

Were we viewed as a couple by the others? And what were Damien's vices exactly? I hadn't figured that out yet. He didn't drink much. He wouldn't smoke weed with me. He drank a fucking green smoothie and worked out every day. What *were* his vices?

Drugs and sex? That was all I could think of.

"Damien's pretty straight laced except for the Molly, right?" I said it in a casual voice, hoping to glean some tidbit I didn't already know.

He had the good graces to look down without answering. He didn't want to talk about Damien's sex life.

We both turned to watch Damien, who was listening intently to something Sydney was saying.

His brow was furrowed. He didn't look happy.

"I mean besides him loving to fuck everything that has a heartbeat, right?"

The man burst into nervous laughter. I gave him another look. No, he hadn't been the one slipping out of Damien's room in the pre-dawn hours.

"Yeah."

I leaned forward, putting my hand on his.

"Or maybe there is something you aren't telling me?"

He squirmed. Suddenly I felt stone-cold sober.

"Why don't you tell me ..." I left the question hanging.

But then the conversation between Damien and Sydney grew heated. So much so that we all shut up. We couldn't help but watch. I couldn't make out what he was saying. His voice was low.

His left hand clenched his napkin. The vein on the side of his neck pulsed.

Damien noticed we were watching and quickly regained his composure.

"Sorry, we just both got passionate about our sports team. I know I shouldn't care that much, but I've been a Raiders fan since I was ten."

Sydney's face remained expressionless.

He raised his hand for the bill.

"I thought we should make it an early night. I've arranged for us to hang glide tomorrow at first light. I wanted to fit it in before the crowds descend on Rio for Carnival."

After he finished speaking, people resumed their conversations, but I kept staring. He met my eyes, and I forced a smile, but I couldn't help but wonder what the fuck had just happened.

CHAPTER FORTY-FOUR–
Dangerous Ground

Sydney lingered after everyone headed for the line of SUV's out front, saying she had to swing by the women's room.

Once she was inside the bathroom, Sydney stood in front of the mirror, clutching the porcelain sides of the sink with her hands, searching her own eyes.

Fuck. He was on to her.

That accident involving Gia today? The tank had clearly been for her. She'd been suspicious and switched it. Which had saved her, but nearly cost Gia her life. If she'd only been more certain that something was awry, she would've made sure Gia's tank was safe, as well.

Well, now she knew.

And while it was a pain to protect Gia when the woman wouldn't believe anything bad about Damien, Sydney would still do it.

But right now, Sydney wasn't worried about Gia, even if the woman was being drugged. Right now, Sydney knew, Damien had his sights set on her. She was his target.

He'd revealed his hand at dinner.

She'd casually mentioned that she'd met one of his employees—a man named Clem. It was a risky move.

As soon as she spoke, she realized just how dangerous a game she was playing.

The name had sparked a reaction that sent a deep chill down her spine. Damien's eyes had turned into black pools without light. Looking into them, Sydney thought she saw death itself. Shaking the foreboding off, she grabbed her glass and took a big sip of her wine. But then set the glass back down.

She had to stay sober. She was on very dangerous ground.

"Tell me again where you met this Clem?" His voice was cold and calculated.

Sydney met his gaze. "I didn't say."

Think fast, Rye. She was scrambling to remember any other Clem she'd ever heard of.

"I don't know anyone by that name." He didn't blink as he said it.

Sydney smiled. "My mistake. I think I was wrong. His name was Daniel. I think I got him confused with Clem Daniels, the Raider football player."

"That fucker?"

The swearing surprised her. Damien hadn't sworn before. That's when she noticed three empty wine glasses and an empty bottle by his place. He was drunk.

He pounded his fist on the table and grabbed her wrist so hard she knew it would leave a mark. Using her other hand, she easily freed herself from his grasp in a well-rehearsed self-defense move that came naturally to her. His eyes lit up with surprise. *That's right, fucker, underestimate me*, she thought.

Everyone else at the table had grown quiet and were watching and listening.

Damien smiled and made an excuse about them arguing over a sports team.

Now, in the powder room, Sydney's hands were shaking. She had to think fast. Now that Damien was on to her, her time was running out.

CHAPTER FORTY-FIVE-
Release

S ydney Rye was endangering everything.
The life he'd crafted so carefully. The persona he'd developed to show the world.

It was his own damn fault. He'd had too much to drink. Bringing her to Brazil was a mistake. But he'd made a worse mistake by overreacting when she'd brought up Clem.

Had he been sober, he would've been able to maintain a placid face. But he had lost it. His anger, thinly disguised, had revealed something to her. He'd seen it in her eyes. What she suspected, he didn't know, but he knew she was on to him somehow.

And she would make him pay.

She was trying to make it all crumble before him.

A mere woman.

Clem. Where in the fuck had she found out about Clem?

In his room, downing yet another whiskey, he chided himself. He allowed himself to indulge on vacation but sometimes, like tonight, he over did it. As soon as he got back to the states, he was going on the wagon again. Intoxication impaired his judgement and made a man weak.

Made a man make mistakes.

Like Sydney Rye. She was a mistake.

She was dangerous. And she'd have to be dealt with.

His entire life hung on the brink of the precipice because of one dumb bitch.

But, like everyone who'd ever crossed him, she'd be sorry. Just like his mother. Just like every other woman who didn't worship him like she should.

She'd played her hand too early. After dinner, he'd made a few calls. He'd found out exactly who she was and who had hired her.

Information on Joyful Justice was scarce, but Damien was able to cobble together a rough idea of what they did and who was involved.

After he took care of her, he'd focus on destroying everyone else involved in the vigilante organization. Just for kicks.

Right before she took her last breath, he'd tell her what he knew and what he had planned. Just to see the terror in her eyes before the light left them.

And then he'd get on with his own life. With Gia.

Picking up the phone, Damien punched in a familiar number.

At first, he argued with the person on the other end of the line and then he realized he'd let the heat of his emotions steer him wrong. This new plan was smarter, more cunning, less risky.

"Get it right this time."

After a few moments, he hung up and logged onto this computer. He brought up a secure dark web website and transferred ungodly amounts of bitcoins into the proper account. He'd pay the second half once the job was done.

The results were worth every penny.

The important thing was that she would be dead by tomorrow night.

CHAPTER FORTY-SIX-
Truce

Early the next morning, yawning and wiping the sleep from our eyes, we all piled into the black SUVs. The road wound through the Tijuca Forest to the top of Corcovado Hill. We would see the monumental Christ the Redeemer statue up close before we headed to a nearby mountaintop to hang glide.

As we drove beneath the dense jungle canopy, Damien told us that the Tijuca Forest was the world's largest urban rainforest. We turned a corner and were greeted by a massive waterfall nestled in the greenery.

"Pull over!" Damien said it so loudly I jumped.

"This, my friends," he said proudly. "is the Cascatinha waterfall."

We got out of the SUV and stood near a small stone wall, admiring the cascading water of the falls surrounded by such thick greenery that the air itself seem to have a greenish, otherworldly light.

The air around us was filled with the drone of unfamiliar, exotic insects. The buzz crested and fell as insects swarmed by us unseen. In the distance, I heard a noise that sent a chill down my back. It sounded like the creature from the movie Predator—and that it was heading our way.

"Howler monkey." Damien said.

"Holy shit."

"Right?" He looked pleased. "That's why we got up so early and stopped here. They only howl first thing in the morning when they wake from the tree they slept in."

The loud clattering of a bird seemed impotent after the Howler monkey sounds. I looked at Damien again.

"Magpie jay."

I nodded as if I knew that already.

We all climbed back into the SUVs, and continued up the mountain on a winding forest-lined road. I kept watch out the window, hoping to spot a monkey, or at the very least, an exotic looking bird. But what I was most excited about was at the top of the mountain.

I couldn't wait to see the iconic statue up close. Ever since I could remember, it was the first thing I thought of when I heard the word "Brazil." My mother had been a fervent Catholic and had talked about wanting to see the Christ the Redeemer statue.

She and my father had joked about "adding it to the list" of exciting trips they wanted to take now that their children were grown and on our own.

But she'd been murdered before that. All their plans were shattered when bullets from a psycho's gun took them away from me. But I'd see it for her. I'd drink in the view she'd so often dreamed about.

I was interrupted from my memories by Damien exclaiming loudly. "We must celebrate!" He leaned over and picked up a small ice chest from the floor near his feet. Laughing as the SUV bumped down the road, he popped the Champagne and managed to make four mimosas without spilling a drop. He handed Sydney hers first.

"Truce?"

She smirked, but took the glass with a nod

Cars were wedged in to every possible spot in the parking lot at the foot of the statue. It was like visiting the Statue of Liberty or the Eiffel Tower. Major tourist overload. Our driver dropped us off at the base of the stairs leading to the statue.

The second half of our group, who had been in the other SUV, stood in a tight circle, furtively passing small pills around. I guess they needed some Molly to enhance their pleasure. Like standing at the foot of the world-famous fucking Christ the Redeemer statue wasn't enough?

"Glad you wore your walking shoes," Damien said, glancing down at my ballet flats.

I shot a look at the rest of our party. Zoe and Cat wore high-heeled sandals. I read a sign about the statue as we waited for them to join us.

I bet those women would have some killer blisters after scaling the two hundred and twenty steps to the top.

That's when I saw them head for a line to the elevator.

I laughed.

The rest of us took the stairs, feeling like cattle as we merged into the stream of people heading upward. It wasn't any better at the top. People stood shoulder-to-shoulder, angling their cameras up at Jesus's gentle features and open arms. At one end of the platform, several people lay on their backs, shooting photos of the iconic landmark. The view was spectacular. The perfect combination of tropical blue seas and lush green hills.

I leaned my back against the small wall and gazed up at the serene look on the sculpted face. I said a silent prayer for my mother and then turned my back on Jesus, looking out over Rio to hide the tears in my eyes from anyone else.

Back down in the parking lot, we got into the SUV and headed for the top of another mountain.

When we arrived at the hang gliding spot, Rich and Damien climbed out and headed over to a king-cab truck parked nearby. Two squat, dark-skinned men stood by it. One wore a beat-up straw hat and the other a well-worn ball cap.

I stretched, doing some half-hearted Budo moves, sucking in the clean mountain air. At one point, Damien walked over to where the equipment rested and was talking intently with one of the men.

After a few minutes, Damien came back over.

"Looks like the fog is dissipating. We should be able to see for miles without any problems. Otherwise we get a full refund," Damien said, shooting a glance toward the two men, who were now standing with their arms folded, leaning against the truck.

Damien directed us to the gliders we'd be using. Sydney started toward a red one, but Damien pointed her toward a black one at the end.

He turned around, and she watched him walk away. The look on her face sent a trickle of foreboding down my spine.

She noticed me staring and lifted her chin to acknowledge me before she turned on her heel and headed toward the black hang glider.

CHAPTER FORTY-SEVEN-
Game On

There was no way Sydney was going to use the hang glider that Thornwell had directed her toward. Sydney had zero doubts that he knew she was on to him. It would make her job a little tougher—maybe even life-threatening—but she'd manage.

Physically, he wasn't a problem. She could take him out in a heartbeat. But until she had proof that he'd done something to Alaia, her hands were tied. If she could track down his *pied-a-terre*, perhaps she'd find the evidence she needed to take him out. And while Schwartz wanted to take care of Damien his way, Sydney knew she'd be the one who'd have to handle it. Thornwell was too dangerous, too powerful, and too wealthy. If he realized what she'd uncovered, he'd be in the wind. He'd create a new life with his scads of money and prey wherever he landed.

When he'd pointed at the black hang glider, Sydney walked over and introduced herself to the pilot.

"I'm Gabriel," the man said. "The owner."

"I haven't done this in a while," she said, casting a glance over at Damien, who was inspecting his own glider. "Is there some type of safety check we should do? I can't remember."

Gabriel smiled. "I checked it myself last night. I took her out for a test run. She is in tip-top shape."

Sydney looked up in time to see Damien watching. He quickly looked away.

"Does Damien usually fly with you?"

The man frowned, lifted his hat, and scratched his head. "Yes. It's a little odd for him to allow a guest to take this glider. He's usually territorial about it."

Casting a sly glance her way, he said, "I figured you maybe were more special than the other ladies he usually brings here."

Sydney nodded. "Yes, I think you're exactly right. I am different than the other ladies he brings here. Which reminds me ..."

She dug into her small backpack and took out the picture of Alaia. "Did you ever see this woman?"

Gabriel took the picture and nodded. He was about to say something, but when he looked up, a strange look crossed his face.

When she saw where he was looking, Sydney understood why.

Damien had stopped what he was doing and was glowering at Gabriel.

"No, I've never seen her before," Gabriel said and thrust the picture back at her.

Sydney bit her lip, thinking.

"Exactly when did Damien decide that I should fly with you?"

"He called last night about nine and said there had been a change of plans. That the blonde lady would ride with me."

"Gabriel, would you mind giving the glider another once over before we take off? I'm a little nervous. It would make me feel better."

Gabriel smiled. *A nervous woman was something he could relate to,* Sydney figured.

"Of course. Anything to make you feel more comfortable."

"Thanks." She glanced over at Damien. He was adjusting something on his own glider. "I'll be right back. I'm going to use the restroom while you give her a once over."

She planned to tell everyone her stomach was upset so she'd have to pass on the hang gliding. But when she stepped out of the bathroom and looked around, she was confused. The spot where her glider had been was empty. She spotted the pilot on the platform at the edge of the cliff.

A scream lodged in her throat as she raced to stop him. She was too late. She watched in horror as the pilot stepped off the platform. The top of the glider dipped violently and disappeared into nothingness. As Sydney ran, her eyes scanned the lot and met Damien's. He was staring at her with an expression of pure fury.

CHAPTER FORTY-EIGHT-
Over the Edge

I wasn't really paying attention to the other hang gliders until my assigned pilot looked up from his inspection, and his face turned a sickly shade of white.

He bolted to the edge of the cliff and peered over. After a moment, he took off his ball cap and crossed himself. With a mounting weight of dread in my stomach, I raced over to join the rest of our group, now gazing down the cliff face from the platform. As I passed my pilot, I saw that he was weeping. I looked over the edge. I could see the black hang glider shattered on the rocks far below. A motionless body was sprawled nearby.

"Oh my God. Oh my God!" Tears pricked the corners of my own eyes.

Sydney brushed past me and muttered something under her breath.

Damien grabbed her arm and yanked her back. Within two seconds, Sydney's elbow had cracked into Damien's lower jaw sending him reeling back. Rich and I stood wide-eyed and open-mouthed as Sydney took off at a run.

The SUV started up. Sydney was behind the wheel. The driver, who had just come out of the bathroom, started to run. Sydney squealed the SUV to a stop in front of me. "Get in."

I froze. What the hell was going on? Before I could react, she sped away, the massive tires spitting up rocks.

"What the fuck was that about?" I said. My voice had a slight hysterical whine to it. "Is he dead?" Damien and Rich didn't answer. They both stared at me wordlessly.

Then Damien grabbed his phone and stepped aside, speaking Portuguese.

The man assigned to my glider came over.

"We must tell police."

"No *polícia*," Damien said. "I've already notified the proper authorities."

We all piled into the other SUV.

When we arrived back at the villa, the other SUV was parked in the driveway. I immediately looked for Sydney, but couldn't find her. Her room was empty. She was gone. So was her dog.

Fuck.

Damien stood in the hall when I walked out of her room.

"I need to be honest with you," he said. "Sydney has accused me of some pretty serious wrongdoings. I've been trying to ignore it. I didn't want to spoil the trip."

"What did she say? What is all this about?"

I put my hands on my hips and stared at him, willing him to answer and alleviate my growing misgivings.

"Nothing. Some untoward business dealings. I think she is angry I chose you over her."

I kept my face blank. He was fucking joking, right? Did he think I was that stupid? Maybe I had been, but no more. I could see through his lies. It was as if Gabriel's death lifted the pheromone cloud that had been obscuring reality.

His eyes grew hooded, and his lips moist. I could see he was becoming aroused. I looked around and couldn't figure out what had caused it, but I wasn't having any of it. He reached for me, but I wriggled out of his grasp.

"I'm sorry." I averted my face so he couldn't read the truth there. "I need some time alone. I'm pretty shaken up. I mean, a guy just died, Damien."

That sobered him up. Or else reminded him that he was supposed to seem distraught.

"You knew this guy, right? Aren't you upset." I was laying it on a little thick, but I didn't care.

Damien pulled away and gave an exaggerated sigh. "You're right. Responsibility calls. I'm supposed to receive the inspector here in a few minutes anyway to go over the accident. Although I don't know what I can say to help their investigation."

I ducked into the open doorway of my bedroom. Before I closed the door, Damien said, "They may need to speak to you, but if I can prevent that, I will. Okay?"

Wordlessly, I nodded.

I shut the door and leaned against it, listening, my heart pounding. After what felt like forever, I heard him move away. I bolted the door and then raced over to the adjoining door to lock it before I remembered he had a key.

I pushed the dresser over in front of the door. It was small and light, but it would stop him at least a little. I didn't know why I needed to barricade myself in my room, but all my instincts screamed to do so.

There was only one person who could tell me if I was losing my mind.

"Dante?" I held the phone to my ear so hard it hurt.

"Gia? What's wrong?" In the background, I could hear the bustle of the restaurant, the clanging of pots and pans, the kitchen staff shouting orders.

"There's some weird stuff going on down here."

There was a pause. "Let me go somewhere private." I waited until it was quiet in the background. "What's up?"

I didn't quite know where to start.

"This woman, Sydney Rye, she is here investigating the disappearance of a San Francisco woman that has had dealings with Rich and Damien."

"Okay."

"Well," I flinched as I said the words. "She thinks Damien is involved."

"In the woman's disappearance?"

"Yes."

"Huh." I could imagine his olive-skinned face scrunched up as he thought about this. "What do you think?"

"I don't know."

"How are things going with you two, anyway?"

I exhaled loudly. "I want to be around him all the time."

"That's a good sign."

"And he sometimes annoys the fuck out of me."

"Normal."

"But I also feel like I need to keep my guard up."

"Does this Sydney have any proof?"

"No. That's what she's trying to get."

"Has he done anything weird?"

I flashed to him with that woman on the beach.

"I don't know. He's a player. Even with me down here with him."

That shut Dante up.

"You sure you want to get involved with a guy like that?" he finally said.

"I'm not ready for a commitment, either."

"Aha." I could hear something in Dante's voice.

"What?" I was wary of what he would say next.

"Gia, are you sure that your unease isn't your natural defense mechanism trying to stop you from falling for this guy? I mean, it would make sense that you are leery of falling in love right now."

Bobby. The name was unspoken, but we both knew what he meant.

I shrugged, then realized he couldn't see me.

"I don't think so," I said.

A booming voice yelled Dante's name. I head the mumble of voices.

"Gia," Dante said. "I've got to go. The duck is charred. I've got to whip something up. I've got a senator from Connecticut in the dining room."

"Call me later?" My voice was plaintive. But he'd already hung up. I flung my phone down on the bed and the flopped down myself, burying my face in my arms.

I felt the vibration of my phone and looked over. My phone was lit up with a text.

Sydney Rye.

CHAPTER FORTY-NINE-
Favela

Settled in to her one-room apartment in the slums of Rio—the favela—Sydney couldn't believe that, even after everything that had happened, Gia still didn't believe that Damien was a killer.

She'd sent a text giving Gia her number and saying she'd come for her if necessary.

Gia had written back.

"Thanks anyway."

And dismissed her.

After ditching the SUV, Sydney headed into a favela not far from Ipanema Beach. All she took with her was Blue and small backpack.

Sydney had done her research well before leaving the states. She knew she'd need a place to go underground if things went south—which, of course, they had.

Named for the thorny favela plant, the slums of Rio—called favelas—had a long history of providing shelter for the down-and-out. Immigrants looking for work took shelter in the slapdash structures that were scattered on the hills on the outskirts of Rio. More than a quarter of the residents of Rio lived in one of the one-thousand favelas in the area.

Leaving the beach community behind and stepping into a crowded street, Sydney felt Blue's nose tap her thigh to show he was sticking close. Drawn by a wide staircase painted with dancing figures on a yellow background, Sydney headed for higher ground. As she ascended, an elderly man with a cane was slowing making his way down to the shopping district she'd just come from.

He didn't even glance her way, which made Sydney realize she'd chosen the right location to lay low.

At the top of the staircase was a small platform leading to a bridge that overlooked the slums. There, two women posed for pictures with the ghetto in the background. They spoke English and were obviously tourists.

A group of teenagers stepped out of an alley nearby. The group surrounded the two women, flicking their hair, herding them up against the rail of the bridge, reaching for the camera.

Sydney waited with Blue in the shadows of a building, waiting to see what would happen.

The group of boys spoke Portuguese and broken English.

Sydney could only make out a few words.

"Camera. Nice camera. Give."

The two women shrank against the rail of the bridge as the boys surrounded them.

Sydney crossed the space between the group with Blue at her thigh. They were no more than a foot away from the nearest boy. They were all so focused on the women and their prize, no one had noticed them yet. Sydney looked down at Blue and gave a quick nod. The guttural sound that rose from Blue's throat made one boy freeze and cock his head. When he turned his head slightly toward the sound and saw Blue, he jumped and propelled himself to the other side of the circle.

Blue's growling turned into a fierce, deafening bark, and the boys scattered with shouts. They raced over to a wall and scrambled up onto it. Once safe, they looked at one another and began to laugh nervously.

Sydney looked at Blue and the barking stopped.

The two women cowered against one another. One was crying.

"Thanks," the brown-haired woman said.

"Let's take one more shot," the other woman said.

"Hey," Sydney said. "Maybe it's not the best idea to be taking selfies with your thousand-dollar camera in an area where people struggle to find food every day. It's disrespectful."

The brunette had the good grace to look ashamed, but the other woman just sneered. "Whatever," she said.

Sydney jutted her chin toward the group of boys who stood nearby whispering and talking. "I'd get back to your little safe hotel before the sun sets.'

The brown-haired woman nodded and turned to the other one. "She's right. Let's go."

Sydney waited until they left before she turned back to the boys.

"Hey guys, want to pet him? He's really a sweetheart. Bark worse than his bite you know."

A few of the boys broke into wide grins and jumped down from the wall. Several crouched down and whistled. Blue looked up at Sydney. She nodded, and he headed their way, tongue lolling and tail wagging.

After a while, Sydney was led to her new apartment by a little girl in a stained dress. She was the sister of one of the boys. The girl led her to an alley and a small doorway, and when she knocked a woman with a bandanna over her hair answered.

At first, the mother seemed afraid of Blue, but when the girl hugged the dog, the woman nodded and let them in, showing Sydney to a second-story small room overlooking the street below.

Sydney gave the girl and her mother several hundred dollars, putting her finger to her lips for them to keep quiet about it. The mother, who looked much older than she probably was, nodded solemnly and tucked the bills into her bra, but not before giving Sydney a wide grin, revealing chipped teeth.

Sydney spent most of the day hunkered down on her laptop or talking to Dan on her cell phone. She needed dirt on Damien and Clem fast.

Finally, Dan called back. He'd hit on something.

"I found the real estate broker for the *pied-à-terre*. He's in Rio."

"Thank God."

Sydney had worried she'd have to fly to another part of Brazil to confront the real estate broker, her only hope in finding Damien's *pied-à-terre*.

She copied down the address and hung up. It was nine at night. Too late to do anything about it. She'd have to wait until morning. But she was ravenous. She called for Blue and left the tiny apartment, then headed to a small neighborhood restaurant where she planted herself at one of the outdoor tables. It was a risk.

If Damien had put word out on the street to look for a blonde with a big dog, she'd be found quickly.

But she was counting on Damien's snobbishness to protect her. He would never consider staying in the favela—the area ringing the hillside above Ipanema Beach. Even though it was near the beach, it was considered the wrong side of the tracks.

After dinner, Sydney headed back to the small room, but took a circuitous route and kept looking behind her, checking to make sure she wasn't being followed. While she was counting on Damien's snobbery to keep her hidden, she realized that was far from a guarantee, and she should keep her guard up.

And it got her to thinking. She had assumed Damien would have a place in an upscale area. But maybe he kept his *pied-à-terre* in the favelas, the slums. Underground. In the city's dark underbelly. He could be anywhere.

After she got back to her apartment and got Blue settled in, Sydney went to bed. The next day would be busy.

IN THE PRE-DAWN LIGHT, Sydney threw on a black windbreaker and grabbed a ball cap to hide her hair. She laced up her sneakers and took Blue for a run along the beach.

Even though she felt pretty safe in the favela, she still set her alarm early, so she and Blue could get in a good run. She felt guilty keeping him cooped up all day in the apartment. Again.

Blue was as eager as she was, so they struck a fast pace heading south toward the more desolate areas. At that hour, they had the entire beach to themselves while the Carnival partiers were still sleeping off their escapades. She was grateful for the solitude and time to think, especially because a blonde woman and her giant, white wolf dog was more than a little conspicuous. At the moment, keeping a low profile would keep her alive.

After the run, she fed Blue, showered, and headed out. Although Blue was bound to attract attention where she was going, she needed him at her side.

In the heart of Copacabana, the shop owners were only beginning to unlock their doors. Men took brooms to sidewalks, and women arranged displays of fresh fruit and vegetables.

She walked past the address she'd written down and staked out a spot at a café table on the sidewalk, ordering *café da manhã* and *pão de queijo* – coffee and French bread with cheese.

The waiter brought Blue a bowl of water and she settled in to wait.

CHAPTER FIFTY-
Vigilante Assassin

"I can't believe it. That was the hang glider I was supposed to be on," Damien said, shaking his head.

I'd squinted my eyes at him, blinking away the sleep.

He'd knocked on my door first thing this morning.

"It's the best hang glider," he said, as if continuing a conversation we'd been having. "Was the best. Gabriel is, God, *was*, the best pilot. I thought I'd make it up to Sydney by allowing her the best pilot and glider."

I smiled, but something about his words was familiar.

That's when I realized. He'd said the same thing about Mario. How Mario was the best diving instructor. How Mario usually instructed him, but he'd hired him for me and Sydney. I narrowed my eyes, but he didn't notice, just kept speaking.

"Now, I know someone is out to get me." He said it matter-of-factly. I drew back. I wasn't sure I'd heard him correctly.

He exhaled exaggeratedly.

"I didn't want to alarm you, but the accident with your tank yesterday? That wasn't an accident. And it was meant for me."

I scrunched up my face.

"Do you see?" He paused and searched my eyes.

I waited.

He ran a hand through his hair. "Someone is trying to kill me."

I remained expressionless. Too many things weren't adding up. But was Dante, right? Was everything I felt and saw tainted by my fear of falling in love? Was Damien the target of some madman? It made more sense that someone was trying to kill him instead of someone trying to kill Sydney. He was a public figure practically.

"That diving tank? Supposed to be mine. The hang glider? The one I was supposed to use. Sabotage."

"Who would want you dead?"

"I don't know." But then he gave her the side-eye. "Maybe Sydney?"

I laughed. "Sydney?"

He handed me his phone.

I read the story three times before handing it back to him.

After her brother was viciously murdered, placid dog walker Joy Humbolt killed the man behind it all. She changed her name to Sydney Rye and was at the core of a powerful underground organization called Joyful Justice that fought against injustice.

The article, on the dark web, said she was a vigilante assassin. That people believed many others had died at her hands. Of course, it also said those murders were justified.

"She's a killer?" I tried to sound surprised and maybe even a little shocked. "Maybe she had good reason."

He guffawed. "To murder? Hardly."

I decided to keep my mouth shut about the people I'd killed. And the fact that some would even call me a vigilante assassin. We could get into all that later. When we knew each other better.

But the fact was that Sydney Rye had taken a life—several lives apparently. Same as me.

That explained the bond I'd felt with her from day one. Not something I was proud of. But it was my reality. What I'd learned today had made me wonder about her. Had she been trying to turn me against Damien? Was she the one trying to assassinate him?

"What were you two really arguing about anyway?" I said. "Maybe it turns you on that she's dangerous."

Damien squirmed and I knew I had zeroed in on it exactly. That weird tension I felt whenever they were around each other."

"It's not like that."

"Well then what is it with you two?"

"We're just haggling over some business stuff. She thinks her company stock is more valuable than I do."

"What is her company?"

"It's called CyberForce." He didn't skip a beat.

"Oh."

"Let's lay low today," he said, reaching over to tug the strap of my nightgown off my shoulder. "Tonight, we have the samba parades and Carnival kick off. It's going to be a long day and late night."

He tugged my nightgown down to my waist and leaned over and kissed me.

My body responded. But at the same time, Dante's words haunted me.

My doubts, my unease, did they stem from my fear of opening up and being vulnerable? Of allowing myself to love again?

Dante knew me so well. He was the closest and longest friend I'd ever had. What if he was right?

I'd wait. Time would tell if my discomfort was justified. Right now, I needed to feel, not think.

CHAPTER FIFTY-ONE-
No Dogs Allowed

The man in the small office took Sydney in, raking his eyes down her body.

Then he saw Blue.

"No dogs," he said in a gruff voice.

"Fuck you."

His eyes grew wide, and his face flushed red.

Fighting the temptation to throat punch him, Sydney instead whipped out her gun, holding it to his temple before he could blink.

"We can do this two ways. You can tell me now, and I walk out of here. Or you cannot tell me and I kill you, draw the blinds, and search your office."

"I don't know what you are talking about."

Sydney brought a well-aimed heel into his crotch. He cringed and reached for his lap.

"Don't move."

"It's not here," he said.

"She drew the gun back a little and tapped his head with the barrel. He kept a straight face.

"Blue."

Blue stood and growled ferociously and then put his snout near the man's crotch.

The man winced. "Okay. Okay. It's at *Calle Montego*."

"Show me. I want to see the paperwork."

"Call off your dog."

Blue backed away a little, but stood on alert.

Darting a wary glance at Blue, the man reached over into a file cabinet and pulled out a manila folder.

"Open it."

Even from a few feet away, Sydney could make out the name Clem and the address.

"Perfect." She jutted her chin toward the bathroom in the corner. "I need you to go in there for a few hours. I'll try to remember to come back and get you, but if not ..."

She trailed off with a shrug.

After locking him in the bathroom, she drew the curtains in the office and put out the closed sign.

CHAPTER FIFTY-TWO-
Samba

We didn't set out until the night was dark.

The SUV dropped us off on a side street, not far from the main drag where the samba parades would happen. The closer streets were closed to vehicle traffic for the night.

Grasping my hand, Damien led me toward the lights and music.

The night was thick with excitement, sex, and music. The entire city seemed to throb with sensuality.

Nearly everyone we passed wore costumes.

The women wore barely there glittery bustiers, and dresses with masks and tiaras and headpieces. The men wore tuxedos or dressed like Arabian royalty or medieval kings.

We turned a corner and were greeted by a mass of people swaying and drinking and laughing. Damien held tightly to my hand as we navigated the crowd. He turned to say something to me, but his voice was lost in the cacophony of music streaming from the restaurants and balconies that surrounded us.

Flesh pressed against flesh as we squeezed through the crowd. The air was thick with the smell of sweat, perfume, and fried foods.

Finally, we stood in front of a small doorway tucked back a few feet from the street. Damien unlocked the door and gestured for me to enter first. I scaled blue-painted stairs straight up to another door, this one painted purple. I waited on the tiny landing as Dante locked several deadbolts behind us. Then he pressed against me as he unlocked the purple door.

"This is where we watch the parade."

I stepped inside and smiled.

The tiny room was done up like an ancient harem.

The largest bed I'd ever seen took center stage. The walls were painted black and the floor was scattered with ruby, emerald, and sapphire velvet cushions.

Across from us, French doors were thrown open to a small balcony.

Candles covered every flat surface. A gust of wind from the balcony made all the candles flicker wildly. "Aren't you worried about fire, having this burn while nobody is here?"

"My caretaker did it. They've only been lit for a few minutes."

"Oh."

A small table held a silver bucket with a bottle of Champagne, tiny drips of moisture condensed on it.

Nearby rested a plate of grapes. A tiny alcove held a galley kitchen with a moka pot on a burner and a small refrigerator.

"This is perfection." I turned to him. He kissed my palm and then walked over to the table with the Champagne. He leaned over and pulled out the bottle of Veuve Clicquot. He popped the cork without a sound.

"I want tonight to be special," he said over his shoulder. "To be perfect. I've waited a long time for this night."

I swallowed. What was going to happen tonight? He turned his back to pour us some Champagne.

I walked over to examine a series of prints on the wall. They were of stunning beautiful naked women.

He grinned and handed me a glass of Champagne.

"This is my secret hideaway. I call it my *pied-à-terre*. I love the parties in Rio. I really do. But I must escape and be my myself at times. It's my personality. All those years spent coding in a garage by myself. My true nature is that of a loner."

I examined him. I was a loner, too. Maybe that was part of the attraction.

I worried I was falling for him. I couldn't help it. But a small part of me wondered if it was pure lust. All I knew is that my body craved his touch all the time. I was in a state of constant arousal. It was ridiculous.

Another small table near the balcony contained other snacks, strawberries dipped in chocolate and an assortment of nuts. The sheer curtains flanking the balcony blew into the room, beckoning me.

I took my glass and moved outside. I pressed up against the cool terra cotta balcony wall, the enveloping night heat embracing me.

Below, a mass of sweaty bodies squirmed, maneuvering down the street, preparing for the parade to start.

In the distance, at the end of the street where the parade began, a half dozen brightly colored hang gliders dropped out of the night sky leaving a trail of fireworks that seemed to spark from their feet. The sight of hang gliders made my throat grow dry. I shot a look at Damien but his eyes were only slit with pleasure.

I turned my attention back to the street below— the pulsing, wriggling bodies laughing and drinking and dancing.

The sound of a shrieking whistle made everything shift and grind to a halt.

The street below suddenly cleared as the thousands of people lining the parade route pushed onto the sidewalks in a crushing mass. Music started up, and the anticipation built.

"About three blocks down there are massive bleachers on each side of the street," Damien said, appearing at my side to refill my Champagne glass. "This block is the first one where the parade weaves through the old part of town. We get an up-close experience. Anywhere else and you are dozens of feet back. This street is so narrow, when the big floats go by, you can reach out and touch them."

"Wow. This is great."

"It's the only way to experience Carnival."

He offered me a joint, holding it between my lips and lighting it for me.

Finally, the front of the parade reached us.

It was led by an astonishingly beautiful woman wearing little more than a bright blue braid of fabric for a G-string that snaked up her body to silver cones covering her breasts. Massive blue-feathered wings spread out from her shoulders. The band behind her was dressed in the same bright blue and wore cartoonish, oversized silver crowns and beat on drums and tambourines and gourds draped in silver chains.

But I couldn't stop looking at the float behind her. It was taller than our entire building. It was comprised of a dozen twenty-foot tall gold bulls and platforms with half a dozen dancers. At the top of the float, a woman in a flowing gold dress floated on water that shot up from inside the float.

I gasped.

"Pretty dope, huh?"

I only shook my head in answer.

Damien wrapped his arm around me and put the joint between my lips again. After I exhaled, I spoke.

"This view. This place. It's amazing."

"I always come here to watch the first night samba parade during Carnival. I've done it every year for a decade."

A small flicker of jealousy zipped through me, imagining all the women he'd brought here before me.

Suddenly, he left, rushing inside. I heard his voice over his shoulder. "Wait. I forgot something."

He came back and handed me a mask. A beautiful courtesan mask with jewels.

Then he strapped on a mask that sent a chill down my spine.

"Wow," was all I could. The mask was basically a white face with a large nose, no mouth, and creepy beak-like chin

"It's a Rio traditional mask called a *bauta*. It is very symbolic. I wear it here every year."

The samba music was mesmerizing. I found myself swaying to the beat, leaning back against Damien's firm body. The beak-like chin of the mask stuck out as he rested his chin on my shoulder.

I was high and horny and in heaven.

The atmosphere of the parade was intoxicating. The air exuded a carnal sensuality that sent electric shocks tingling from my scalp to my toes. At the same time, the heat and the rhythmic music and the weed made me feel languid.

As we stood there, Damien nuzzled my neck sending chills down my limbs. He took my palm and opened it, placing a tablet in the center.

It was like the other pills I'd seen, but it was pink.

Molly.

"Just this one time?"

I stared into his eyes. I was already so fucking high. My inhibitions were already nil. Why not? It would just enhance our lovemaking.

I searched his face. His eyes were soft, and I saw something in them that I would swear was love.

"Turn it over."

At first I was confused, but then he looked down at the pill in my palm. I took a finger and flipped it.

Stamped on it were three letters. GIA.

I looked up at him.

"I had them specially designed and flown down yesterday."

His voice was slightly muffled by the mask.

I stuck out my tongue. He placed the tablet on it. I swallowed.

He twirled me around so my pelvis was pressed hard against the terra cotta wall of the balcony. He pressed himself against my back. Hard.

I could feel every ridge of his manhood on my spine and lower back. I pressed back against him, overcome with desire.

As he spoke into my ear, his voice sounded odd from the mask.

"Today we are strangers," he said. "We just met on the sidewalk below. I've brought you here to fuck you."

I pressed my body back against him and moaned. The Molly was starting to make me feel incredible. I was up for anything.

He lifted the back of my dress as another samba school started. I felt the rhythmic throb and vibration of the drums over every inch of my body.

Damien stood and suddenly was inside me. There were thousands of people only a few yards away, but they were all below us. Nobody could tell what we were doing. Besides, the mask made me feel invisible.

With Damien moving inside me, I stared at a woman from a samba school on the street below.

She had perfect ebony skin. Her flesh looked like velvet. Only small gold stars covered her nipples, connected to gold chains that led up to her neck and down to her belly button. On her head was an elaborate gold and white feathered headdress. Her eyes were lined in deep kohl. Her entire body slick with a metallic sheen of sweat. She wiggled her hips, and the samba band behind her followed suit as she gyrated and moved the parade past us.

Damien breathed four words into my ear. "I love you, Gia."

He pulled me into the bed with him. I was wild with desire. As we made love, I stifled every small alarm or negative thought that tried to enter my conscious. I deserved to love and be loved, and all the zingers of fear were old patterns, old records that told me that everyone I loved died.

Dante was right. I was so terrified to lose another person I rejected love.

This time it would be different.

THE SAMBA SCHOOLS WERE still passing by when I got up, tugged on a silky robe, and snuck to the bathroom. Damien had fallen into a deep sleep almost immediately after we made love. Usually he was not like that. Normally, he was still attentive to me, rubbing my back and stroking my hair. He must be worn out today.

In the bathroom, I closed the door so the light from the bathroom wouldn't wake him. I took off my mask and squinted at the light as I threw cold water on my face. Examining myself in the mirror. I smiled. I was happy. I was satiated and happy. But also, high. So fucking high.

Was this love? It felt so different than what I had felt for Bobby. My love for Bobby was comfortable, natural, like another part of myself, a warm, cozy blanket on a cold night. My love for him was soothing and felt right, as if there was nobody else on earth for me.

With Damien, I felt as if I might die if I didn't see him every day. Instead of warm and cozy, it felt like a wild, dangerous ride. An addiction. Dangerous but irresistible. The most exciting adventure I'd ever been on.

I rummaged for a toothbrush and toothpaste in my overnight bag. Damn. I'd forgotten the toothpaste back at the villa. I was sure Damien had some. I cracked the medicine cabinet. As I did, I realized that the drug had affected my vision.

Everything was shiny and bright. Earlier when I peeked in, the bathroom had seemed shabby and even a little dirty. Now, it sparkled. Everything glowed and glinted. It was a side effect of the pills.

I found the toothpaste in a drawer, and when I put my toiletry bag back down on the counter, I missed. The bag tipped over, sending its contents clattering onto the tile floor.

I froze. Had the sound woken Damien? I listened but didn't hear him stirring in the other room. I leaned down to pick everything up, brushing it to one side and scooping up containers to put in my bag.

One of the bottles had rolled back behind the toilet. The building was old, so in some places the walls didn't meet the floor and there were small crevices. As I crouched and reached for the bottle, something glimmered in one of the spaces, catching the light. It was pink and sparkly.

I nudged it. It didn't come out. I got out my tweezers and pulled it. Then I dropped everything. The tweezers fell with a clang.

It was a fingernail. A bloody fingernail. With a small rhinestone set in hot pink nail polish. The nail was ripped.

It was the same as the fingernails I'd seen in the photo that Sydney had showed me of Alaia.

He'd taken the missing girl here.

Time stopped. I stared at the nail. My face grew icy and yet sweat dripped down my temple. My hands were trembling. I was suddenly freezing. My entire body shook with cold.

Noises seemed amplified. The dripping faucet in the tub thudded and echoed loudly. The vibration of music from the street pierced my bones. The whirring electricity emitted from the bare bulb hanging above me penetrated my brain.

I heard the floor creak outside the bathroom, somewhere in the other room, and it was as if an alarm had gone off in my head.

Heart pounding, I scrambled to my feet, scooping up the fingernail in my palm just as he entered the bathroom. His mask hung loosely around his neck. I vaguely remembered yanking it down there so I could get to his mouth.

"What are you doing?" His voice was stern. The sweet tone from earlier had disappeared.

"I was looking for toothpaste."

Something about my voice alerted him. His eyes grew dark.

"You dropped the tweezers."

Leaning down he scooped them up. I held my breath.

He stood and examined them carefully. I tried to keep my face blank but knew the horror I felt inside was seeping through.

"What have you been getting into while I was asleep, Gia?"

My eyes darted to the door. He didn't miss any of it.

CHAPTER FIFTY-THREE-
Wait and Watch

G ia had come out on the balcony alone at first.

Then Damien had joined her, pulling on a mask.

Sydney lost view of the balcony just as the first samba school started.

The crowd had grown as dozens more people filed into the narrow street. Despite her best efforts to fight against it, Sydney was caught up in the tide and ended up two blocks down. She'd have to circle back around if she wanted to keep an eye on the *pied-à-terre*.

Her fear was that Damien would leave the apartment alone. But she wasn't sure enough to actually break into the place. For now, she would wait and watch.

CHAPTER FIFTY-FOUR-

Monster

I had to make him think I wasn't a threat. That I was weak and debilitated from the drug. Okay, I actually was a little bit, but I could exaggerate it.

First, I had to swallow the fucking heartache that threatened to make me scream and cry. How could somebody I'd fucked—no made love to—be a monster. How could I have been so blind.

Goddamn it all.

"Out." He gestured with his chin toward the bedroom. I slipped past, keeping my hand in a fist, hiding the fingernail.

He followed me and then stood between me and the door.

"I don't understand why you're so mad?"

His eyes narrowed. It was if he was battling with his emotions about whether to believe me. "Gia? What were you doing in the bathroom?"

"I told you."

The fingernail was still tightly clenched in the palm of my hand. My arm was down at my side.

His eyes went right to my closed fist.

"What's in your hand?" Damien grabbed my wrist. That's when I saw that his other hand held a knife. A long, shiny butcher knife. My

eyes involuntarily flickered toward the small kitchen island. A knife was missing from the wooden block.

Holding the knife to my throat he ripped open my palm. The fingernail fell to the floor.

He leaped back as if it were on fire.

His face grew red and he panted loudly.

I watched, terrified. It seemed like I'd never met this man before me. Violence suffused his entire body, transforming him into a stranger.

He didn't say a word. But his eyes rose from the fingernail to my face. Before I could react, he had thrown me on the floor. I instinctively curled into a ball but not before he got a solid kick into my ribs.

I gasped in pain.

"Get up."

I scrambled to my feet.

With one hand still on the knife, he grabbed a giant roll of plastic and gestured toward the bed. "Help me put this on the bed."

The horror of that plastic was replaced by irrational anger. "No."

"What?" He actually seemed surprised by my refusal.

"I'm not one of your victims, Damien. I'm different. You know it. I know it."

"I thought you were special," he said. "But now that you know, you have to die. I won't ever stop. I thought I could love you and continue my lifestyle, but I see that was a foolish dream."

He did think I was special. That was my advantage. That is how I would get out of here.

"Damien," I said, making my voice soft. "We are soul mates. I don't care if you killed someone. I've killed people. Did you know that about me?"

I spoke as fast as I could. I was still on the floor. I wanted him to look down on me. Think of me as weak and ineffectual because of the drugs I'd taken.

He drew back slightly. "What are you talking about?"

"Don't tell me you didn't research me."

He shrugged.

"You know I've killed before, right?" I said it in a rush. This was my chance. I took a deep breath. "I've killed. And I've liked it."

"What?" Now his face was really scrunched up.

"I've been looking for someone to share that with. For so long. And now I've found you."

I held my hand out to him for him to pull me to my feet. I held my breath, waiting. This would determine everything. If he believed me. If he bought my lies, I had a chance. If he strapped me to that bed, I was done for.

I wasn't sure how I'd be able to fight him when I was seeing double, but I knew I'd have a better chance standing.

Reaching down, he yanked me to my feet, but instantly sprung back with the knife. Still wary.

"I realized something tonight when we were making love," I said, moving toward him, my eyes locked on his.

He cocked his head. His body tense. It looked as if he would spring forward and attack any second. The knife in his palm was steady, aimed my way.

"What did you realize?" His voice was calm. But the look in his eyes revealed his curiosity. He'd not expected this. Not one bit. He needed to believe me. I needed to say it and mean it. In some way.

I swallowed. "That I love you."

I reached toward him and stroked his cheek with my fingertips. He closed his eyes. The tension drained from his body, as if it had deflated. The arm holding the knife dropped to his side.

"But that doesn't mean I won't make you pay for what you've done," I spat, arching up and lunging for the knife. I grabbed his arm with the knife and turned the blade toward him. He managed to twist the knife out of my grasp and it dropped to the floor at the same time my head came up and cracked his chin. The blow sent him flying back. I swiveled, moved forward, and planted a foot into his chest, sending him reeling. Then I aimed for his crotch. He crumpled, howling in agony.

Knowing I only had seconds, I raced to the door and fumbled with the deadbolt, my heart racing like mad. I could feel him behind me, struggling to get to his feet. Finally, flinging the door open, I raced down the stairs. At the bottom, I started undoing the three deadbolts, the hairs on the back of my neck standing up straight as I heard the wooden landing at the top of the stairs creak.

"Gia. Get back here. You don't want to leave. If you do, I'll be forced to kill you."

At that second, the last deadbolt slid open. I yanked open the door as I heard the terrifying pounding of him racing down the stairs after me.

Instantly, I blended into the crowd on the sidewalks, imagining him at my back, yanking my hair to pull me toward him. Fighting and pushing through the bodies, I hoped I was gaining ground, putting space between us. The music was deafening, so I couldn't hear anything as I wove through sweating, costumed bodies. As I passed one woman, much shorter than me, I ripped the mask right off her head and strapped it on my own face.

I kept running. I dodged in and out of crowds as the samba music throbbed around us and fireworks exploded overhead. Hands clutched at me, touching me intimately, caressing me, tugging at my silk robe, sending shocks of fear down my spine as I imagined the cold steel of Damien's knife slicing through my skin.

At one point, the parade had stopped in front of me. Everyone clapped and danced in time to the samba school. While I tried to force my body between the dancing spectators, I turned my head, glancing back behind me for the first time. Through the other bodies, I saw his creepy masked face clearly. He'd pulled his mask up onto his face. Even so, I could tell his eyes were wild. Dangerous. Blood lust had overtaken him. I saw the blade of a knife in his hands glint in the streetlights.

I ducked, scrambling low to try to hide as I made a sharp turn that took me close to the buildings instead of the street. Glancing behind me I saw him coming steadily toward me. Then I saw that a small wall blocked my way ahead. I turned and in an alcove, saw a doorway. To the right was a passageway. But it could be a dead end.

I was trapped.

He knew it. He slowed down. He would stab me in the crowd. Nobody would know. And then he'd be gone. Nobody would even be able to hear my scream. But I had no choice. I turned halfway toward the passageway, turning to see how close he was behind me.

As I did, I felt cold steel on my neck.

At the same time, now only five feet away from me, Damien froze.

His eyes were fixated at something over my shoulder. His look was filled with hate. Slowly, trying not to take my eyes off him, I tilted my head, trying to see what was behind me using my peripheral vision.

I couldn't see anything. I was too afraid to take my eyes off Damien. But then to my surprise, he backed up and disappeared into the crowd, ducking in front of a huge float that took up the entire street. The cold steel left my neck.

I whirled around.

Sydney stood there holding a gun at arm's length in front of her.

When I caught her eye, she winked.

CHAPTER FIFTY-FIVE–
Brainwashed

Damien, that murderous motherfucker, slipped away in the crowd. At first Sydney stepped forward, ready to give chase, but reason stopped her. He had too much of a lead. He'd taken advantage of the float and used it to escape.

She'd get him another way.

On her own terms.

Gia was now at her side, reaching down to scratch behind Blue's ears. "So, happy to see you pretty boy," she said.

Blue, who was between the two women, licked Gia's hand and then nudged Sydney's thigh.

The music grew faint as the samba school moved past.

"Let's find him and kill him." Gia spoke without looking at her.

Sydney didn't answer.

Turning on her heel, Sydney cut across the street quickly, keeping an eye out for Damien, but if her hunch was right, he'd fled, putting as much distance between them as possible.

Gia was close behind her. Sydney ducked into an alley way and then, after looking behind them and seeing nobody in pursuit, turned again quickly.

It was only when the samba music had dwindled, that she stopped.

"He's in the wind," she said. "Let's find something to eat and figure out where he might be."

They entered the favela. The streets were darker. Few people were out. Everybody was at the parade. But one restaurant had a few café tables on the sidewalk and a bright light on inside.

Sydney pulled out a chair and sat. The owner came out and stood before them.

"We'll have whatever you want to bring us," Sydney said. The man smiled and disappeared back inside. "And beer."

Gia collapsed into the seat beside her. "I need some strong coffee or something to sober up. He gave me Molly."

"You mean he offered it, and you took it?"

Gia nodded, rolling her eyes. "Yeah. Stupid." She put her head in her hands. "Everything. Everything I've done since I met that man is stupid. I feel like I've been brainwashed, living in a cult and only now has the fog lifted so I can see reality. So fucking stupid."

Sydney reached out and put her hand on Gia's arm. "He was giving you something to make you feel that way. I can't prove it yet, but they're called love pills. You've been drugged. I think we need to take you to see a doctor."

Gia rolled her eyes. "Would you go to the doctor in my case?"

Sydney slowly shook her head no.

"Exactly."

Sydney hadn't heard the thunder or seen the lightning since she'd come to Rio, but that didn't mean it had gone away for good.

"He's a fucking charming, manipulative motherfucker," Sydney said. "How do you think he's made it to where he has?"

"But he's a murderer, isn't he?"

Sydney shrugged.

"But then again, so are you," Gia said, her eyes trained on Sydney's face.

Sydney smiled and said, "Takes one to know one."

For a few seconds, Gia looked astonished, but then she smiled.

The owner set a beer before them and Sydney took a slug.

"We don't have time for a pity party or an analysis of where we've gone wrong," she said. "We have to find him and stop him before he disappears for good."

"What?"

"Dan traced some conversations, texts, emails. Damien made a huge wire transfer out of a Swiss bank today. I'm talking $50 million dollars. He's going underground."

"Holy shit. Well how can we find him before he does?"

Sydney shrugged.

"I'm sure he's not going to back to his little *pied-à-terre*," Gia said, frowning.

They sat in silence for a few seconds, and then Gia spoke again. "I feel like I can't trust myself. That feels terrible. I was so certain I was right about him and you were wrong."

"If the drug does what I think it might, a lot of this, hell, most of it," Sydney said, "was probably out of your control."

"I'm just so angry."

And probably heartbroken, Sydney thought.

After she went inside and paid the owner twice what he asked, Sydney led Gia back to her small apartment.

Once inside, Sydney opened up her laptop. She typed in a flurry. Gia sank on the couch, holding her head in her hands.

"I have a fucking headache from hell now, too."

"Yeah, Molly does that to some people and who knows what kind of withdrawal symptoms you might get from that drug," Sydney said.

"I haven't been drugged." Gia's voice was adamant, but Sydney could hear the slightest hint of doubt.

"Listen," Sydney said. "Let's brainstorm. We've got to find Damien."

"What if he's already left the country?"

Sydney typed some more and looked up. "Nope. His plane is still here on the ground. That's a good sign for us."

Sydney scooted back her chair and turned to Gia.

"Come here. I want you to meet Clem Smith."

Gia stood and stretched. "Who?"

But when she looked over at the laptop screen, her face grew pale.

Sydney could tell that even from across the room Gia could see the faces on the screen. She hurried over.

"You've got to be fucking kidding me."

There were two pictures on the screen. One of Damien Thornwell taken some time in the past few years. Next to it, was a mugshot of Damien as a teenager or young man. It had a Sheriff's identification strip underneath it. An arrest photo for Clem Smith. He had light brown hair with a receding hair line and bad teeth.

Underneath the photo was a headline: "Youth charged with raping classmate and murdering mother."

Gia stared at the screen and then said, "Holy shit, he has false teeth and dyes his hair."

Sydney burst into laughter. Gia joined her until she had tears streaming down her face.

Finally, they stopped. Gia wiped away her tears. "I guess I had to laugh so I didn't cry, but ended up bawling anyway. This is so fucked up. He raped his classmate, and a few years later, killed his mother after she threatened to go to authorities with proof of the rape."

"And changed his name."

"Motherfucker."

Sydney nodded. "Exactly."

"I always thought it was sort of creepy that his name was so similar to the devil in The Omen?"

"What?"

"You know in that movie with Gregory Peck? He plays the devil—a guy named Damien Thorn."

"Fucking creepy."

"We found something else."

"We? You mean that Joyful Justice?"

"I had unsolved rape cases in the Bay Are run through our data base and found several with similar M.O.'s—women who had some connection to Sky Enterprises. But I also found something really interesting."

Sydney scrolled through a file. "The classmate he raped was named Lila. In at least two rapes after that, the victim said her attacker sobbed and said, 'I hate you Lila. I hate you.'"

"He's repeating whatever happened with this Lila, and somewhere along the line it escalated to rape and murder," Gia said. "Can we find Lila? Can we have her publicly identify Damien as Clem? Is there DNA evidence? I know the statute of limitations is expired, but we could somehow bring attention to him, even if we can't prove he killed Alaia, we can make others aware of him, warn other women ..."

Gia trailed off. Sydney slowly shook her head.

"He's fucking Damien Thornwell."

Gia clasped her hand over her mouth. "Oh, my God. You're right. Nobody will believe us."

"We have to do something," Sydney said. "He'll never stop. Even if he goes underground, he'll continue raping and killing women. Sexual predators don't just stop. Ever. We have to stop him."

The two women stared at each other for a few seconds and then both nodded.

"Let's do it," Gia said and headed for the door.

CHAPTER FIFTY-SIX-
Orgy

After sleeping much of the next day, we headed out to the villa under the cover of night. My head still hurt like a motherfucker, but I was eager to find Damien. I wanted to make him pay for what he had done. I wanted to look into his eyes and hurt him. With my words and actions and fists, just like he'd hurt me.

We circled the house, coming at it from a parking lot down the beach and then lay down in the sand out back.

Sydney handed me her night vision goggles.

"Tell me what you see while I talk to Dan. It's on heat seeking. Flip this to switch to night vision."

I strapped them on and peered up toward Damien's room. The full-length windows made it easy to see inside from our vantage point.

Sydney was talking in a low voice on the phone to someone named Dan who was at Joyful Justice headquarters.

It was dark inside Damien's room, and I didn't see any movement whatsoever. I scanned my room. Nothing.

Two rooms over though, I saw bodies moving.

The bodies were entwined. I switched to night vision and zoomed in. Zoe and Cat and Nick were having at it. Wait. Tim was also there, half buried under the covers. Good for them.

But no Damien.

A glance at Rich's room told me there wasn't anything there, either.

Downstairs, I scanned the common spaces. Thank God these people didn't believe in curtains.

Nothing.

All the fun was happening at the orgy upstairs.

"Where the fuck is Rich?" I said.

"There's something I have to tell you," Sydney said as she hung up her phone.

I dropped the glasses and turned to her.

"Dan's been monitoring the police frequencies. While you were sleeping today they found Rich."

"And?"

"He's dead. They found him in Damien's *pied-à-terre*. They found a knife and a gun near his body. Shot himself. Both had his fingerprints on it. They found a prostitute's body in the closet. Stabbed. She'd been there for a few days. It was staged to make Rich look like the killer."

Bile rose to my mouth. I'd fucked Damien with a dead woman's body a few feet away. I don't know how, but I knew who the woman was. The woman I'd seen Damien with on the beach. But I had to ask.

"What did the woman look like?"

Sydney exhaled. "Honestly? Like you. Fucking spitting image."

I leaned over and vomited.

"We don't have time for that shit."

I swiped at my mouth and nodded.

"Wait? How do you know what she looked like?" I asked, but already knew the answer. "You went there today while I was asleep?"

Sydney nodded. "It was the second time I'd been there. I was there last night before you arrived, but the caretaker had come in and I'd had to hide under the bed until he left. That's how I found you. I'd been keeping an eye on the place and saw you rush out and Damien chasing you. I went back today to search for the notebook."

"You searched while the prostitute's body was there? And Rich's body?"

She cleared her throat. "It wasn't a pretty sight. Anyway, Alaia's last text said her notebook would be there, but I couldn't find it. I thought the notebook would provide evidence, but he might have found it and destroyed. He has to be stopped. With or without evidence. We need to trap him. I'm just trying to figure out how."

"She spoke about a notebook?" I sat up, remembering my conversation with Damien about his commonplace book.

I keep a notebook that contains details of my life...I have it with me at all times.

"What if it is his notebook, not hers," I said and told her about the commonplace book.

Her eyes widened. "That's what we need to find. It has to have evidence. But meanwhile, we need to find him and stop him."

Suddenly it hit me. "I know! The Wizard's Ball at the Copa? He has to attend. He's the master of ceremonies. His ego won't let him miss it."

Sydney's voice held a grin. "I don't think my running shorts will blend in."

I took her arm. "Let's go shopping."

CHAPTER FIFTY-SEVEN-
The Dog, Too

Damien paced the penthouse at the Copacabana, his phone to his ear.

"You have to make sure that every security guard within ten blocks of here knows that there has been a threat to my life. I want roadblocks two blocks out and each vehicle checked. Unless they have a ticket, turn them away. I don't care if it's the goddamn actress who won the Oscar this year. Ticketed guests only. Do you understand?"

"I'll take the private elevator down, give my speech, and then I'll require an armed escort up to the helipad on the roof immediately after."

Damien hung up and dialed another number.

"I leave at midnight. I want them both dead. And the dog, too."

CHAPTER FIFTY-EIGHT-
Rock and Roll

Figuring that shopping for dresses after the Carnival festivities had begun was near impossible, Sydney knocked on the landlady's door and thrust a large amount of cash toward her. Within an hour, a man appeared at their door with dresses and masks. He left with enough money to probably pay his rent for two months, and Sydney and Gia decided to try to nap before the ball.

At nine-thirty, Sydney woke Gia.

"Time to rock and roll."

Gia stretched. "Thank God, my headache's finally gone."

After they dressed—Gia in black, Sydney in white—they put on the jeweled eye masks.

Sydney handed Gia a small black bag on a silver chain. Gia took it and felt its heft. She looked inside and saw a small automatic pistol.

"You know how to use that?"

Gia nodded.

"It's a Sig Sauer P238. It's my spare. But it will work." Sydney patted her own bag and smiled. "I'm fully loaded."

They waited until they saw the big black car pull up on the street below before they left, Sydney patting Blue on the head. He looked at her dolefully as if he knew he might not ever see her again.

The landlady had been instructed to call Dan if Sydney didn't return.

Dan had helped them form a plan. He'd hacked the website of the firm providing security for the event.

According to Dan's information, checkpoints would be set up around the hotel. And the ballroom would be heavily guarded. Inside, guards would be posted at the main entrance and exit and one on each side of the stage.

Dan had also sent blueprints and they'd studied plans of the ballroom before their nap. The stage Damien would appear on was against a far wall, opposite the door.

They would wait in the wings and then each approach, one on each side of the audience, and take him out at the podium. Dan had helped Sydney find an elevator just off the stage that would take them either to the basement or a different floor. From there, they'd separate and meet in the kitchen. Sydney hoped that once there, they could dress like cooks and escape in a catering van. But it was risky. A lot depended on the level of surveillance throughout the hotel. If they could get out of the hotel, they'd ditch the van before the checkpoints and head back to the *favela*.

AFTER HANDING SYDNEY the keys, the driver slunk off into the shadows.

I'll drive," Sydney said, lifting the lid to the trunk.

"What if I suffocate?" Gia said.

"Then bang on the trunk lid."

Gia crawled in with a scowl.

"Hey," she said once she was lying down. "Can we drive Cameron Stone? I think I have a crush on him. I'm pretty sure he likes me, too. He was staring at me at dinner the other night. How about we pick him up instead?"

"No." Sydney slammed the trunk, pulled down her chauffeur cap, and climbed into the driver's seat. She immediately cranked the stereo, blasting Cuban music. The sound was interrupted by a muffled banging.

Sighing, she got out and peered into the trunk.

"You can't breathe?"

"Just testing."

Sydney rolled her eyes and slammed the trunk lid.

CHAPTER FIFTY-NINE-
Pity Party

Lying in the dark, I wanted to kick the lid of the trunk. Why the fuck was I the one stuck in this suffocating, smelly space? Whatever rich fuck we were driving to the ball would probably love having two female chauffeurs, right?

I hadn't realized I was slightly claustrophobic until now. My breath came in rapid, shallow gulps. I was certain I would hyperventilate. It took all my willpower not to kick and scream for Sydney to let me out.

I did some deep breathing and felt a little better. I had no choice.

The two of us together would draw attention we didn't want or need.

Any reports of a livery car with blond and brunette drivers would get back to Damien. I was sure of it. At worst, we'd be killed. At best, we'd be banned from the ball and wouldn't be able to get to Damien. And that was all that mattered. Getting close enough to do some real damage.

My bag was pressed against my hip as I lay in the trunk on my side. I patted it. The gun was small but would work.

We went around a sharp corner and I slid, banging my head on the inside of the trunk.

"SLOW THE FUCK DOWN SYDNEY!"

I slipped off my sandals and aimed one bare-footed heel at a tail-light until it came loose then I curled up in the fetal position and wriggled until I'd managed to turn my body around.

I jabbed at the tail light until it loosened. If I held it a certain way, I could see out about an inch. For some reason this made me feel better. Less claustrophobic. Less trapped. And I'd see who was coming. And if it wasn't Sydney, I'd be prepared.

I reached for my bag and felt the reassuring weight of the gun inside. I pressed the fabric of the bag, feeling the outline of the lethal steel. My fingers itched to hold the gun and squeeze the trigger. I visualized Damien up on a stage and me rushing up and facing him, holding the gun outstretched between us.

I imagined the look in his eyes. Astonishment. Betrayal. Hurt. Love.

Love. Fuck. Swallowing hard I closed my eyes.

He loved me. I knew this. I was certain.

Could I kill someone who loved me? Yes. The hard part was going to be killing someone I loved back.

Because as fucked up as it was, it was true. I both hated and loved Damien. For my entire adult life, I'd lamented that everyone I'd ever loved had died—most in terrible and violent ways. I'd spent countless hours living in fear that if I loved again, the object of my affections would end up dead. And yet here I was stuffed in the back of a trunk during Rio's Carnival, mentally preparing myself to put a bullet through Damien's head.

We rounded another corner, and I braced myself this time, preventing another head whacking.

I heard a muffled voice say, "Sorry."

But I imagined Sydney smiling, taking the corner a little too fast on purpose.

I knew she was frustrated that I hadn't believed her about Damien. But she'd only seen his bad side. I saw the other side of him. The sweet side of him. The humanity in him. The tender look when he made love to me. The side of him that loved that goddamned dog, Snuffles. The part of him that had given two million dollars of his money to a pet rescue organization we saw on TV one night.

The Damien that was first interested in my company because he had a soft spot for the homeless. I remembered him stopping to talk to the homeless man outside my building and how it was genuine and real and how he treated that man with respect and dignity.

But *that* Damien was dead.

Besides, his name wasn't even Damien. It was Clem.

And Clem was a monster. A stone-cold killer. A predator. A depraved waste of flesh who preyed on innocent women. Who abused his power to indulge in his sick perversions.

I clenched my jaw. *That* Damien/Clem must die.

We came to a stop, and I heard voices and doors opening and shutting.

Our client.

Somehow Dan and Sydney has arranged for us to drive some muckety-muck to the ball. We'd drop him off at the red carpet and then, instead of parking where all of the other chauffeurs were designated to sit out the ball, Sydney would make up some story allowing us access to the hotel garage. We hoped.

After a few minutes, we slowed. I peeked out my tiny hole and saw cars behind me. We must be at the checkpoint.

We were getting closer to Damien.

Steeling myself, I pushed back the memory of the last time we made love. But not before I remembered the look in his eyes. I quickly replaced that thought with another one: Alaia fighting for her life so hard that her entire fingernail ripped off her finger. I imagined the prostitute's dead body slumped in the closet mere feet away from us making love.

I clenched my fists. He must die.

And at my hands.

I was the reason that woman on the beach was dead

If I'd only listened to Sydney, I would have realized he was a killer. I would have known to warn that woman, and she would still be alive. Maybe a pill had something to do with making me more vulnerable and allowing my lust and emotions to overpower my logic and good sense, but the fact of the matter was someone had died because of me. Never again.

Damien needed to die. And I needed to be the one to do it.

The car ground to a halt again. This time I heard the distinct clicking of the paparazzi and saw the flashing strobes through my gap in the taillight.

Then we pulled away. Before we turned a corner, I got a glimpse of a crowd pressed up against the fence overlooking the red carpet.

Sydney parked in a far corner of the garage and sprung me from my prison.

I brushed off my dress and leaned over strapping my heels back on.

"There was a reason I gave you the black dress," she said, helping to brush off my back.

"Um, because black is my color, obvi," I said.

She smirked. Then her face grew expressionless. Her gray eyes met mine.

"Ready?" she said.

I searched her eyes for a second before answering, "Let's do this."

We stared at one another for a second and then headed toward the elevator.

CHAPTER SIXTY-
Carmen Miranda

The elevator doors slid open to a room aglow with purple light. The twenty-foot high doors to the ballroom lay directly across from us. As we made our way over, my stomach grumbled as we passed tables of filet mignon, shrimp scampi, and hamburgers.

At the doorway to the ballroom, Sydney and Gia paused.

"Look," Sydney said and pointed inside at Gia's celebrity crush, Cameron Stone standing talking to a six-foot-tall, ninety-pound model in a skintight dress. He looked hot. She looked...hungry.

Everything was glittering and dripping gold—the costumes, the jewelry—even the Jurassic-Park-sized bees and butterflies hanging from the ceiling. The room was bathed in a red glow. The walls were covered with red velvet drapes and red lights shone down upon the writhing crowd.

Women wore sparkling gowns. Many sported elaborate dazzling tiaras or feathered headdresses. One woman was dressed like Cleopatra. Another like Carmen Miranda.

Most of the men wore tuxedos. But a few had dressed up: Aladdins, complete with turbans, black-eyeliner, and dangling earrings; a sailor, a King Tut.

Sydney saw familiar faces— Zoe, Cat, Nick, and Tim, but they looked right through the two women, not recognizing them in their masks.

Spotlights swam through the crowd, and the band on the stage at the far end played an Indian tune with dancers swaying to the sultry music.

Sydney jutted her chin at Gia and headed toward the right side. Gia made her way toward the left side of the room.

A man in a jester costume and mask grabbed Sydney by the waist and gyrated. She stopped herself from taking him down, so she wouldn't attract unwanted attention, but gripped and twisted his wrist so tightly, that he sprang back and held it in his other hand, cringing.

She continued wending her way through the crowd to the wall.

After evading a number of outstretched, groping hands, she was nearly to the wall when the music stopped dead. Everybody stood still. The band on the stage slipped through the door on the back wall of the stage. The same door they'd planned to escape through. Sydney tried to catch sight of Gia across the room, but the crowd was too thick. The doors to the ballroom were flung open and another band trailed in. The women clicked castanets, and the men pounded on tambourines with drum sticks while the band leader kept time with the whistle in his mouth.

The crowd parted to let the band through to the stage, and people clapped along to the beat.

With everyone focused on the center of the room, it opened up the area by the walls and Sydney was able to quickly make her way forward. A few feet away from the stage, a bulky guard packing some serious heat stood near the steps to the stage. An AR-15 hung loosely against his tuxedo from its straps.

Sydney drew up to a sudden halt in front of a long table stacked with fruit, shrimp, sushi, and other finger foods. She plucked a glass of wine from the tray of a passing waiter. She would stage here until it was time.

CHAPTER SIXTY-ONE-
Liquid Courage

Through the mass of wriggling bodies, I could see Sydney in her white dress. Her blond hair pushed back behind her ears. Her red lipsticked lips pursed as a drunk man stumbled her way. With a swift movement, she twisted the man's arm. He winced in pain and took off nearly at a run, glancing fearfully back behind him.

She smirked.

I drained my Champagne glass and looked around for another waiter. Sure, I was seeking liquid courage. After all, I was about to kill a man who had kissed every inch of my body.

Blessedly, the music came to a halt, and a tall man dressed in African garb complete with a two-foot headpiece took the microphone.

"Welcome! I am Antonio Federaz, the owner of the Copacabana Palace. This is our twenty-fifth year hosting the Wizard's Ball, and I must say each year the event gets better and better."

People burst into applause and cheers. "I'm going to turn the emcee duties over to a good friend of mine. You all know him. He's going to be the first man to live in space. Let's take advantage of having him here this year because next year, he might be living in a luxury home orbiting the moon."

The crowd burst into laughter. I winced. *Or he could be living some-where raping and killing more innocent women.*

"Ladies and gentlemen, Mr. Damien Thornwell."

The door behind the man opened, and Damien stepped out. My heart leaped into my throat, and I suddenly felt like I was going to vom-it.

Zoe and the rest of Damien's gang were front and center to cheer on their benefactor. I shrank back, pressing against the wall, hoping they wouldn't turn and see me.

Out of the corner of my eye, I saw Sydney weaving through the crowd, getting even closer to the stage. I took a deep breath. But my feet were firmly planted on the plush carpet. Move, goddamn it. I closed my eyes for a second.

Do this.

Then I was moving forward, not taking my eyes off Damien.

All sound disappeared. I could see his mouth moving. I knew he was speaking into the microphone, greeting the guests and cracking jokes. I could tell from the smiling, laughing faces around me, but I'd lost the ability to hear. Instead, a pulsating, buzzing filled my ears.

The weight of the gun thudded against my thigh as I walked.

My eyes were laser-focused on Damien's. I watched him scan the crowd. He was hiding it, but I could see the fear in his eyes as he searched the mass of bodies in the ballroom. He was looking for me. I knew it. Me and Sydney. He squinted, and I realized that because of the spotlight beaming down on him, he was having a hard time seeing any-one except the people gathered directly in front of the stage.

I stuck to the shadows near the wall as a bright beam of a search-light swung through the crowd, bouncing from head to head, illumi-nating, laughing, drunk, or masked faces.

Then I was at the side of the stage, not far from the hulk of the guard holding the assault rifle. His back was to the corner of the stage, his unmasked eyes inspecting the crowd. I paused, waiting.

A man charged toward the front of the stage yelling something about terrorists and some other mumbo jumbo I couldn't make out. I could tell in a heartbeat, he was harmless. Loony, but harmless.

The guard reacted instantly, charging toward the man and jerking him out of the crowd and off to the side by me. I put my hand to my chest, acting mortified.

Screams filled the ballroom. Damien stopped speaking and cowered behind the podium.

Instantly, several other men were on the protestor and I made my move. Without waiting to see what Sydney was doing, I yanked my dress up to my thighs and ran. Amid the screams and chaos, nobody noticed me at first.

Except Damien.

His mouth formed an "O," and he shrank back.

He dropped the mic. By the time I had the Sig out of my bag, he'd started to turn. I kept the gun pointed down and pressed to my thigh out of sight. Even so, I fully expected to hear the rat-a-tat-tat of the assault rifle as it pounded bullets into my back.

Right before I leaped onto the stage, I brushed past Stone, knocking into him. "Sorry," I said and winked at him as I vaulted onto the stage in one fluid motion.

Then Sydney was there too, up on the stage with me, and we were converging on Damien from both sides. The door behind him slid open, and Damien disappeared inside the black rectangle.

I raised my hands above my head just as I saw the guard aim the AR-15 at my head. I glanced over and saw that the other guard had a gun pressed against Sydney's forehead. That's when I saw Zoe staring at me wide-eyed, her mouth open.

"Drop your weapon. We are Mr. Thornwell's protection detail. Ask her." I jutted my chin toward Zoe.

She looked confused. Her brow creased, and her eyes were as wide as moons behind her mask.

"Zoe, damn it, tell him we are Damien's personal bodyguards."

She finally spoke. "Yes, they came with us from San Francisco."

The guards lowered their guns. I tried the door where Damien had gone. It was locked.

I turned to the guard. "Where does that door go?"

"The roof."

"Can you unlock it?" Sydney asked.

The man shook his head.

"Follow me," he said. Sydney and I leaped off the stage and followed the guard through another door into a hall where he unlocked a door and stuck a key card into the slot. "This will take you to an elevator to the roof. I have to return to my post."

Slumping in the elevator, I ripped off my mask.

Sydney did the same. She seemed unruffled, but stood rigid. "We're too late."

"Maybe not," I said.

The elevator door opened onto a vast blackness, pierced by the shimmering lights of Rio in the distance.

I swiveled my head, searching the darkness of the roof for movement.

The helipad stood empty about twenty feet away.

I felt the throbbing vibration of the helicopter in my bones before I actually heard the thumping of the rotor blades. It appeared out of nowhere, a black hammering in the night, whipping the air around us, lashing my hair around my face. As I tried to push my hair back, Damien darted out of his hiding place behind an HVAC unit and raced toward the helicopter.

I raised my gun, but my damn hair blinded me again.

A long triangle of light spilled across the roof from a stairwell doorway near the elevator, and a gunshot rang out. For a split second, I thought it was Sydney firing at Damien until I saw her hit the deck. Thank God it wasn't the assault rifle, just a plain old pistol. But still.

In one smooth movement, I was lying beside her, my gun pointing toward Damien.

We were sheltered by some type of rooftop vent.

Sydney glanced at me. "Cover me. I'll take out Damien."

I shook my head. "No. You cover me."

"Are you sure?"

"This is something I need to do."

I'd realized earlier that it was my job to take care of him. I couldn't live with the knowledge that the prostitute had died because of my denials of Damien's true nature.

I could barely see Sydney's eyes in the darkness, but I saw her nod.

"On three," she said.

At her count, she spun and leaped up, firing a volley at the man in the doorway. At the same time, I scrambled to my feet and raced toward the helipad.

CHAPTER SIXTY-TWO-
Delusional

Damien and I reached the helipad at the same time. He was hunched over to avoid the whirling helicopter blades and reaching for the handle of the helicopter's door. My forearm came down on his with a crack that could be heard above the thumping of the rotor blades. He howled and reeled back in pain. I took my heel and swept his feet out from under him. Something he was holding went flying. I was hoping it had been a gun or weapon. He landed hard on his back, but was up within seconds, coming at me.

One blow struck my cheek. It sent me spinning back for a second, but I planted my feet and came at him again.

The popping of gunshots by the roof door made me swivel my head. Sydney. Before I could see what was going on over there, Damien had yanked my arm behind me and had his chin pressed deep into my clavicle. Damn. His legs wrapped around mine, disarming any kick I might have thought about. It felt as if my arm were about to snap in two, but I still struggled against him. His breath was hot against my ear.

Rio stretched out before us, glittering in the deep velvet night sky.

"I loved you," he said. His voice was heavy with anger and betrayal.

"Fuck you," I spat.

"I really thought that I could stop with you by my side."

For a second, my heart stopped beating. He thought he could change? Stop raping and murdering for me? He was delusional. "People like you don't stop, Damien. You're a predator."

I strained to see Sydney. We were facing away, but in my peripheral vision, I could see movement in the light from the doorway. I couldn't tell if it was Sydney or the gunman.

"You made me forget about all of that."

"Is that why there was a dead prostitute in the closet while you were fucking me?"

"I had to get it out of my system one last time."

"You're pathetic."

"Get in the helicopter with me. We can go away. Nobody will ever find us."

"You'll never change. We've already told everybody about you. You can't escape, Damien. You might as well give up now."

"I don't want to escape."

"What about your transfer of funds?"

He burst into laughter. "That's for my attorney and publicist. There is nothing you can do to hurt me or my reputation. They're already creating photographs and evidence that you two were terrorists and that I was your target."

We couldn't fight against Damien and his million-dollar marketing machine. But we might have one card to play.

"I found the notebook." It was a bold-faced lie.

His entire body grew stiff. His demeanor changed. Fear raced through me. He yanked on me. I couldn't figure out what he was trying to do and then I realized he was trying lift me up into the rotor blades. I fought against him. The rotor blades would make mincemeat out of me. Not a way I wanted to go, that's for sure.

I swallowed. He crouched down ready to push me up.

At the last second I went limp, saying a silent prayer that I hadn't just signed my own death warrant. But it worked. When I went limp, he lost his grip on me. I slid out of his arms, grabbed him around his thighs and thrust him upward. He easily escaped my grip and came at me with a blow to my head that sent me reeling. He came after me again, but this time I was ready. I leaped up and landed a jump kick on his chest that sent him flying. It wasn't until I fell to the ground that I realized my kick had propelled him into the rotor blade at the rear of the helicopter.

He died without a word. But his death was not silent. The sickening sound of metal on bone and flesh wasn't nearly as bad as the bath of blood and brains that showered down on me as I sat crumpled on the helipad.

CHAPTER SIXTY-THREE- Going Home

Sydney yanked Gia up and thrust her into the open door of the helicopter.

Hopping in the front seat, Sydney held her gun to the pilot's forehead.

"Get us the fuck out of here. Now."

The pilot's eyes looked straight ahead. "Got it."

The helicopter lifted into the air.

"Take us to the airport."

Sydney turned to Gia. "Get my phone out of my bag and dial the last number I called. Tell them to get Blue to the airport pronto."

"Get Blue to the airport immediately," Gia said into the phone.

THE PILOT FOLLOWED Sydney's directions and set the helicopter down in a private portion of the airport.

After climbing out, Sydney—still pointing the gun—leaned into the open door.

"Who do you work for?"

"Anyone who hires me."

"You own this bird?" she asked.

"Yes." His voice shook.

"Do you know Damien Thornwell?"

"Not really."

"If I let you go, what happens next?"

"I keep my mouth shut?" He sounded afraid.

"That's right. What else?"

"I never saw you?"

She reached over and ripped out the cord that connected to his headset and tossed it out onto the tarmac. "Listen. Don't get cute. You don't owe anybody anything. Tell anyone who asks that you were kept hostage for a few hours and you dropped me off at the other airport. Wait here for twenty minutes and then go home."

The man nodded.

She lowered the gun. Gia and she ducked and ran toward a plane waiting nearby.

"Do you trust the helicopter pilot?" Gia asked once the car doors had slammed.

Sydney shrugged. "It doesn't matter. We'll be long gone before he can put it all together."

The driver drove to a small plane—a jet.

Blue was at the top of the stairs in the doorway of the jet. A woman in fatigues stood next to him.

When she reached the doorway, Sydney leaned over and kissed the pilot on the cheek.

"This is Daniela. An old friend and a damn good pilot," she said to Gia.

Sydney reached down and scratched Blue's ears.

Gia reached for the pilot's hand, but Daniela shrunk away. That's when Gia looked down and noticed the blood and guts caked on her hands and dress.

Sydney tossed her a towel. "Wipe the guts off your face and neck and then sit back and enjoy the ride. Get comfy. We're going home."

Within seconds of boarding, the plane took off, reaching high into the sky.

CHAPTER SIXTY-FOUR-
Coffee and Cornettos

I'd never been so damn happy to be greeted by a huge scruffy dog licking my face.

Django hadn't left my side since Sydney had dropped me off earlier, saying she was going to go check on Damien's dog at his house. I wondered what story she would give the dog sitter.

After the door closed on Sydney, Django had followed me to the bathroom, staring at me as I washed my face and brushed my teeth. He stood at my side as I stripped out of my bloody, brain-splattered clothes and stepped into the shower. I peeked out the shower curtain, and he was standing there staring at me. Shit. I'd traumatized my own dog.

When I dried off and dressed and hopped into bed, he crawled in beside me, resting his head on the pillow beside me, his bulk pressed tight against mine.

The next morning, with the sun pouring in the windows, Django leaned over and licked my entire face.

A noise from the door sent him leaping out of bed, the deep roar of his bark echoing through my loft. The door opened, and his bark disappeared. His entire body wriggled wildly as he greeted Dante. I'd texted him late last night to let him know I was back in town.

"*Paesano*, I hope you have coffee," I said, sitting up.

"And cornettos."

"God, I love you, Dante."

"I know. I know."

I headed toward the table and grabbed one of the two lattes that Dante plunked down. I sipped the creamy coffee greedily as he unpacked the brown bag of pastries.

We didn't bother with plates, just set the pastries on the paper and began breaking off bits.

"Oh, here." Dante thrust a newspaper at me.

"What's this?"

"Cat Woman?" he said with an eyebrow arched and a smirk on his face.

"What?" I was oblivious.

"Inside front."

I turned. The local section contained a small story about a melee at Carnival. It didn't mention Damien's death. I lifted an eyebrow as I read.

"Why don't they have anything about Damien or Rich's deaths?" I had called Dante from the plane the night before.

"I made some calls," he said.

Damien still had connections to Washington. His husband, Matt, had been a senator.

"They claim they are still trying to confirm the identities, but really there is some major damage control being done. On a really high level. Brazil officials are flying into D.C. today. They don't want all those millions of dollars in tourist money gone before the big money-making day. And on our side, they need to come up with some cover story how two of the nation's most prominent citizens died in a friendly country. I can guarantee you most of the negotiations are being done so it doesn't look like a terrorist attack. Carnival makes too much money for that type of publicity."

"Well, they're still fucked," I said. "Right? Won't it hurt business next year?"

Dante shook his head. "No way. The memory of the rich and fa-mous isn't that long. They'll have moved on to some new scandal by then. Keep reading."

That's when I go to the part about the two mystery women.

One in black. One in white.

The reporter interviewed people who were at the ball.

"This guy was a terrorist and he was going to blow us all up."

I looked up at Dante.

"Keep reading."

"Two women hired as protection stopped the man. They were be-ing lauded by ballgoers as heroes."

"You're fucking kidding me."

"Keep reading dammit."

That's when I got to the part he wanted me to read.

It was a quote by Stone.

"She was hot," he said. "Like Cat Woman. And she winked at me. She had a mask on, but she winked at me. I'll be her Batman any day she wants."

"That is hilarious," I said.

"He's just as delicious in person, right?"

"Scrumptious."

"I can arrange an introduction," Dante said.

"Fuck that."

"At least his name doesn't start with a D."

I shoved a huge piece of cornetto into my mouth right when he said it. I wasn't going to answer that for the world. Besides, Damien's real name was Clem.

AFTER DANTE LEFT, I headed up to the roof to soak in the sights and sounds of my beloved city. For once, the fog had departed early, fill-ing the rooftop with glorious sunshine and blue skies.

I stretched, did some Budo moves, and then sat back in a lounge chair under my grape arbor. It wasn't noon yet, but I leaned over to mix myself a drink and fished out a smoke from my secret stash.

Thinking of Damien, I clinically examined my feelings.

I'd loved him—in a really strange way. But I felt no sorrow about his death. He was too damn evil to mourn.

Puffing on my smoke, I exhaled and then sat up and swore, startling Django.

I knew where the notebook was.

CHAPTER SIXTY-FIVE-
Fast Friends

Sydney and Gia stepped out of the rental cottage on the beach. "Let's take a walk." Sydney headed for the boardwalk.

Blue and Django and Snuffles raced along the sand beside them. The three dogs were fast friends.

"What are you going to do with Sniffles or whatever the dog's name is?" Gia asked.

Sydney had picked up the dog from Damien's house the night before after she dropped Gia off.

"His name is Snuffles."

Gia turned to her. "You took a big risk going to his house last night. Why'd you grab the dog?"

"I have a soft spot for him."

"Got room on your plane?"

Sydney shook her head. "I'm a one-dog woman."

Gia ran her fingers through her hair. "Fuck. I guess he's mine then."

They watched the dogs running and playing, darting into and out of the lapping waves on the beach.

"He is cute," Sydney said.

"Yeah, but I've learned not to fall for a pretty face."

"Unless you take love pills that is?"

Gia glared but then burst into laughter.

"I'm glad we got that notebook."

"Me too," Gia said.

Dan from Joyful Justice was already in Rio. He'd been able to search the penthouse, but it wasn't until Sydney called him that he searched the roof and found the notebook in a backpack behind an HVAC system.

Gia had remembered something went spiraling off the helipad when she was grappling with Damien. At the time, she thought it might be a gun or weapon.

When she remembered that Damien always had the notebook with him, she knew.

Somehow during their struggle, it had been kicked off the helipad and sent spiraling behind the HVAC system where it had lodged in a small cubby under a larger platform.

Dan had flown the book to San Francisco himself. The three of them had poured over the details and taken pictures before sending the book onto the proper authorities.

The commonplace book listed details of every single one of Damien's crimes. Every rape. Every murder. His creation of the love pills. His plans for the brain-computer interface. And details of how he and Rich lured female victims with the promise of funding their projects. Then Damien did the dirty work, killing the women and liquefying their bodies in vats of acid in the *pied-à-terre*'s closet. The *coup de grâce* was when the two men stole the woman's ideas, claiming them as their own.

For fifteen years, the two men had been building their company's fortune in this way. More than thirteen women were believed to be victims of the two men. Unfortunately, their remains had been disposed of. The caretaker was arrested, but he pleaded innocent to knowing what he'd been disposing of. The only proof authorities had come from the details in the commonplace book.

Alaia's father, Mr. Schwartz was working to make sure all the families of the dead women received the profits from the ideas the women had brought to Sky Enterprises.

It was justice of a sort.

Gia reached into her bag and brought out a beat-up silver flask. She took a slug and handed it to Sydney.

"Day drinking, are we?"

Gia shrugged.

Sydney took a drink and then examined the flask. The initials GVS were carved into the metal, and it was dented in several places.

"What's the V for?"

"Valentina."

"You could probably afford a new flask."

"This one has sentimental value."

"I figured."

"I gave it away once. But the morgue later gave it back to me."

Sydney eyed her new friend. Because that's what she was. Gia had been through some shit, too. Maybe Sydney had finally met someone who got it. Got it on the same level as she did.

Or maybe not.

At the very least they were friends.

Sydney held up the flask again in a toast this time. "I think this is the start of a beautiful friendship." She sipped and handed it back to Gia.

Gia paused, looking at Sydney. "I should warn you, I've had shit luck with female friends."

"That's too bad. Good women friends will have your back for life."

Gia nodded. "I've heard that. I could use a friend like you. Too bad you live on some island."

Sydney shrugged. "That doesn't matter. You need me, I'm here."

Gia smiled and lifted the flask. "Same."

Sydney saw a black car pull near the boardwalk boarding the beach.

"Listen, I've got a flight to catch."

"I think I'll hang here for a while," Gia said. "I'm meeting an old friend. Plus, I've got some things to think about. Like how I'm never going to be weak like that again. This damn dog," she pointed at Snuffles, "will be a living symbol of my resolve to never be blinded by lust ever again. To never be weak and foolish like that again."

"Hey, give yourself a break," Sydney said, opening the door of the car.

After she and Blue settled into the back seat of the car, they watched Gia sit on the sand, facing the ocean, her knees drawn up to her chest. Snuffles and Django frolicked in the surf. The sun glinted off the water as it rolled into shore. That's when Sydney saw a man approaching Gia. He wore a police uniform.

"Stop the car," Sydney said. After all this, they were going to arrest Gia? She had to do something. But then as the man's shadow fell upon Gia, Django rushed over to the man and put his paws on the man's chest, licking his face. When the dog sat back down, Gia stood, brushed sand off her, and fell into the man's embrace, burying her face in the man's chest.

Sydney smiled.

"Farewell," she said. "Until our paths cross again."

Want more Gia?
Day of the Dead (Gia #7) will be out Nov. 2, 2018.

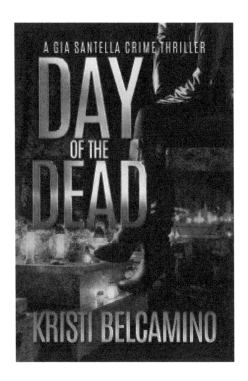

To keep up to date on new releases and special giveaways, sign up for my newsletter here: https://www.subscribepage.com/KristiBelcamino and receive the GIA prequel as a special thank you gift.

Not available for sale anywhere.

Author's Note:

LAST YEAR I HAD THE great fortune of discovering the super talented Emily Kimelman and her terrific books. I devoured the Sydney Rye series and became a fervent fan.

A few months later, I was delighted to meet Kimelman (virtually) and we discussed the idea of me writing a book where Gia and Sydney Rye joining forces to do what they both do best—seek justice for those unable to do so themselves.

Honestly, at first I was a little intimidated by the idea of writing someone else's character, but my excitement about the idea overwhelmed that uncertainty and I'm so glad it did.

This book is the result. I hope you love it as much as I loved writing it.

If you want to chat after you've read the book, you can email me or you can find me on my Facebook group page. It's called Crime, Coffee, & Cannoli. It's the easiest place to reach me. I'm there every day, several times a day. In addition, it's a great place to meet and interact with a bunch of kick butt readers just like you!

In addition, Kimelman has a very vibrant community on Facebook as well. You can find enthusiastic readers and all sorts of cool contests and posts at her group. It's called Emily Kimelman's Insatiable Readers.

We both frequently offer deals on Bookbub so that's also a good place to find us.

Thanks again for reading about two fierce, independent women who won't stand for injustice in any form.

ABOUT THE AUTHOR

KRISTI BELCAMINO IS an Agatha, Anthony, Barry, & Macavity Award-nominated author, a newspaper cops reporter, and an Italian mama who makes a tasty biscotti. As an award-winning crime reporter at newspapers in California, she flew over Big Sur in an FA-18 jet with the Blue Angels, raced a Dodge Viper at Laguna Seca and watched autopsies.

Her books feature strong, fierce, and independent women facing unspeakable evil in order to seek justice for those unable to do so themselves.

Belcamino has written and reported about many high-profile cases including the Laci Peterson murder and Chandra Levy's disappearance. She has appeared on Inside Edition and her work has appeared in the New York Times, Writer's Digest, Miami Herald, San Jose Mercury News, and Chicago Tribune. Kristi now works part-time as a police reporter at the St. Paul Pioneer Press. She lives in Minneapolis with her husband and her two fierce daughters.

Find out more at http://www.kristibelcamino.com[1]. Find her on Facebook at https://www.facebook.com/kristibelcaminowriter/ or on Twitter @KristiBelcamino.

---

1. http://www.kristibelcamino.com/

Made in the USA
Middletown, DE
25 March 2024

52063550R00139